DATE DUE

sammy keyes

AND THE showdown in sin city

Also by Wendelin Van Draanen

Sammy Keyes and the Hotel Thief
Sammy Keyes and the Skeleton Man
Sammy Keyes and the Sisters of Mercy
Sammy Keyes and the Runaway Elf
Sammy Keyes and the Curse of Moustache Mary
Sammy Keyes and the Hollywood Mummy
Sammy Keyes and the Search for Snake Eyes
Sammy Keyes and the Art of Deception
Sammy Keyes and the Psycho Kitty Queen
Sammy Keyes and the Dead Giveaway
Sammy Keyes and the Wild Things
Sammy Keyes and the Cold Hard Cash
Sammy Keyes and the Wedding Crasher
Sammy Keyes and the Night of Skulls
Sammy Keyes and the Power of Justice Jack

◆ ◆ ◆

Shredderman: Secret Identity
Shredderman: Attack of the Tagger
Shredderman: Meet the Gecko
Shredderman: Enemy Spy

◆ ◆ ◆

The Gecko & Sticky: Villain's Lair
The Gecko & Sticky: The Greatest Power
The Gecko & Sticky: Sinister Substitute
The Gecko & Sticky: The Power Potion

◆ ◆ ◆

How I Survived Being a Girl
Flipped
Swear to Howdy
Runaway
Confessions of a Serial Kisser
The Running Dream

sammy keyes

AND THE showdown in sin city

by WENDELIN VAN DRAANEN

ALFRED A. KNOPF
New York

THIS IS A BORZOI BOOK PUBLISHED BY ALFRED A. KNOPF

Visit us on the Web! randomhouse.com/kids

Educators and librarians, for a variety of teaching tools,
visit us at RHTeachersLibrarians.com

Library of Congress Cataloging-in-Publication Data
Van Draanen, Wendelin.
Sammy Keyes and the showdown in Sin City / Wendelin Van Draanen. — 1st ed.
p.   cm.
Summary: When youth sleuth Sammy Keyes travels to Las Vegas to stop her mom from marrying her boyfriend's dad, she never expects she'll learn the identity of her absent father in the process.
ISBN 978-0-375-87053-8 (trade) — ISBN 978-0-375-97053-5 (lib. bdg.) —
ISBN 978-0-307-97408-2 (ebook) — ISBN 978-0-307-93061-3 (pbk.)
[1. Fathers—Fiction. 2. Identity—Fiction. 3. Mothers and daughters—Fiction.
4. Las Vegas (Nev.)—Fiction. 5. Mystery and detective stories.] I. Title.
PZ7.V2857Sapm 2013
[Fic]—dc23
2012013474

The text of this book is set in 12-point Galliard.

Printed in the United States of America
January 2013
10 9 8 7 6 5 4 3 2 1

First Edition

This book is dedicated to Berto and Betty van Veen,
rare saints in a world with plenty enough sinners.

*

With special thanks to:

Mike Clawson, special event supervisor, for taking us behind the
scenes at the House of Blues Las Vegas—your time and patience were
greatly appreciated!

Robyne Wilson and Danielle Meyer, wedding coordinators at Vegas
Weddings, where a bride can walk in, drive through, or do the whole
nine yards.

The security screener at the Clark County Detention Center, who
will remain unnamed, as I already got him in trouble once.

Loraine and Bill "we've never done Vegas like this" Simpson for
sleuthing chapels, rooftops, jails, concert halls, and the back corridors
of Las Vegas with us during the research phase of this book.

Also, thanks to my husband, Mark Parsons, for always being willing
to "talk plot" and for putting the best spin on my harebrained
schemes, and to Nancy Siscoe for her editorial wisdom and support in
reaching this pivotal point in the series.

sammy keyes
AND
THE showdown in sin city

PROLOGUE

It's been more than two and a half years since my mother left me with Grams so she could move to Hollywood to become a movie star.

Or, at least, the Gas-Away Lady, and then a recovering amnesiac in *The Lords of Willow Heights*—a soap so popular it's just been canceled.

Yeah, it's been more than two and a half years since she promised me she would get settled and send for me "soon," but after about a year of broken promises and non-answers it finally sank in that I'm just a burden and an unwanted embarrassment—someone she wishes would just go away.

Or at least quit asking questions.

Especially questions about who my dad is.

But I have a problem with non-answers, and I have a problem with people who don't keep their promises. So when the call came from Casey, I snapped.

Enough, as they say, is enough.

ONE

Casey Acosta is my boyfriend.

He's also my archenemy's brother, and my mother's boyfriend's son.

So yeah.

It's complicated.

Especially since my boyfriend's mother hates me and *my* mother for "stealing her men." Never mind that Candi and Warren Acosta had been divorced a long time before my mother came into the picture, or that Casey's only fifteen and not exactly *property*—we've still "stolen her men."

Now, if anyone's got a legitimate complaint about my mother being with Candi's ex, it's *me*. I mean, there are a billion other men out there for my glamorous mother to choose from—why Casey's dad?

But that's the way Lady Lana is. Grams may hate that I call her that, but I think it sums her up perfectly. She acts like royalty and doesn't care how what she does affects other people. For example, she doesn't think, Whoa, if I marry Warren, his evil daughter, Heather, will become my daughter's stepsister. Or, Hey, my daughter's boyfriend will become her stepbrother! How awkward!

No, she does what she wants and justifies it by telling me that Casey and I can't possibly last. That no relationship formed in junior high school does. That what she and Warren have is *real* and *mature* love . . . not just some silly "junior high crush."

Even though Casey's now a freshman in high school.

Anyway, since there seems to be no reasoning with wannabe royalty, I've just been hoping that her infatuation with Warren will blow over. Or that Warren will realize that he's in way over his head. My mom can be very . . . *snippy* when things aren't going her way, and since Warren was also on *Lords* and they're now both out-of-work actors, well, let's just say warning signs should be posted:

CAUTION: ENTERING SNIPPYVILLE
SLOW DOWN!
TURN BACK WHILE YOU CAN!

It's not like I obsess over them being together. I'd short-circuit if I did. Plus the two of them are way off in Hollywood, and I've got enough worries right here in Santa Martina. Like sneaking in and out of Grams' apartment every day, since it's for seniors only and totally against the law for me to be living there. Or like surviving junior high school. That alone takes major concentration and endurance, but with Heather Acosta lurking around every corner, it's like fancy-dancing through a minefield.

I've got Heather in half my classes—history, science, and drama—and then, of course, there's before school, break, lunch, and after school. And on a typical day, Heather greets me with a sneer and "Hey, loser," or "Outta my way, loser," or "Nice shoes, loser"—that last one being about my torn-up high-tops, which I'm hoping can last to the end of the school year.

True to form, Thursday during third period Heather went toward her seat and said, "Loser," as she passed by. She was texting, so I guess one word was all the multitasking she could handle. Plus she had a red paper clamped under her arm, so she was probably also distracted by her "Love Connection" results from the Valentine's Day fundraiser the school was doing.

Everyone at school had filled out a survey in homeroom. It had questions about what you like to do, your favorite band, your best subject . . . stuff like that. The surveys were put into a computer, and that morning the results had gone on sale. For five bucks you could get a list of the top five people of the opposite sex that the computer thought you were most compatible with.

Everyone was buying their list, but I hadn't. It used to be that spending five bucks on five names would have been out of the question, because Grams is on a really tight fixed income and I don't get an allowance, let alone lunch money.

But for once I was flush. To make a long story short, I'd gotten a share of a big reward for finding a stolen statue, so five bucks was totally doable. But I hadn't bought mine because the whole computer match thing seemed kind of creepy.

Like I can't figure out who I like on my own?

And besides, I'm not looking.

I've got Casey.

Sure, I was tempted out of curiosity—just to see who was on the list. But I got over that when I saw what happened to other people.

Things got . . . awkward.

Like a lot of people, my friends Marissa and Dot bought theirs before school, and when Marissa tore hers open, she whimpered, "Noooo."

"What?" I asked, moving in to see her list.

"How can Jacob Hogan be number one?" There were tears in her eyes. "And Rudy Folksmeir is number two?"

Not that long ago Marissa would probably just have laughed this off, but she's been an emotional wreck for months. In addition to boy problems, I think what's really got her completely stressed out is her parents. They used to be rich-rich-rich, but then they lost a fortune in the stock market and Marissa's father started gambling to try to make up for it.

I'm talking fly-to-Las-Vegas-and-get-rip-roaring-drunk gambling.

And even though he's joined Gamblers Anonymous and has tried to straighten things out, things are definitely not straightened out. Because of his gambling, they're "upside down" on their mansion of a house and may have to move. And last week Marissa's mom caught Mr. McKenze playing blackjack online.

So much for Gamblers Anonymous.

Anyway, Marissa's gone from rich-rich-rich to completely broke, and she's gone from going out with Billy

Pratt—one of the most popular guys at school—to having icky Jacob Hogan and Rudy Folksmeir in the top two slots of her Love Connection list.

"Hey," Dot told her. "Maybe you just don't know them very well. Maybe they're actually interesting and nice."

Marissa gave her a completely defeated look. "Rudy's favorite topic of conversation is *dirt*."

Which is true.

He's *way* into dirt biking.

Marissa leans over to look at Dot's printout. "So who did you get?" And even though Dot pulls back quick, Marissa sees enough to get upset. "You got *Billy*? There's no way you and Billy are compatible! You're quiet, he's a ham. . . ." She flings her arms in the air and shouts, "We want our money back!"

Dot, though, doesn't seem to want her money back. She just wants Marissa to pipe down. "Shh! It's not even anybody's business that we bought them, okay?"

"I have a question," I throw in. "If somebody's on your list, are you automatically on theirs?"

Marissa gasps. "I hope not!"

Our friend Holly has also just been standing quietly by, but since I've piped up, she does, too. "But it makes sense, doesn't it?"

Marissa whimpers, "So right now Jacob and *Rudy* are thinking we're compatible? What if one of them asks me to the Valentine's dance? What am I going to do?"

Holly shrugs. "Say thanks but no thanks?"

Dot adds, "Or just tell him you're going with your

friends." She looks around at the rest of us. "We're still planning to do that, right?"

We all kind of nod, 'cause that's what Marissa had talked us into. And even though it would be fun for me to go to a Valentine's dance with Casey, his psycho mom has forbidden him to see me, so a school dance is not exactly someplace we can meet.

Especially since Heather was sure to be there.

Instead, Casey and I had agreed to meet on Saturday for a Valentine's Day picnic at our secret spot—the graveyard.

Anyway, Marissa's still all worried, saying, "But . . . what if they *go* to the dance and *ask* me to dance?" She wags her Love Connection sheet a little and gives us a pleading look. "They're not the type to buy these, right?"

But it seemed like *everyone* was the type. Or, at least, couldn't resist. By lunchtime on Friday, red sheets were everywhere, including poking out of Holly's back pocket. Only the corner was showing, but there was no mistaking the color.

"You bought yours?" I whispered, giving it a little flick.

She slapped at her back pocket. "Shoot."

I laughed. "It's not a crime, you know. Anybody good?"

She hesitated, then gave me a little smile. "Preston Davis?"

I smiled back. "Oh!"

"But now everything's weird! I can't even look at him without blushing." She rolled her eyes. "Is that stupid, or what?"

Which made me glad I'd resisted curiosity and not bought mine. *Everyone* was getting at least a little wigged out by their results—like they didn't know how to act around their friends anymore because they'd shown up on their Love Connection list.

And that's when I saw Heather pacing around, talking on her cell, waving a red paper in the air. "She's had hers since yesterday and she's *still* talking about it?" I laughed. "I wonder who's on her Looooove Connection."

Holly chuckled. "Five poor schmucks who'd better hide quick."

"Or run fast!" Marissa added.

Dot shook her head. "Can you imagine?"

But then during science I noticed that Heather was texting under her desk. And I don't care *who's* on your Love Connection list, it can't be so bad that you risk texting during Ms. Rothhammer's class. She is strict and she always follows through with detentions, referrals, and confiscations. Everyone knows her rules are ironclad, and when it comes to cell phones, it's real simple: text in class, lose your phone.

And believe me, if there's one thing Heather doesn't want to lose, it's her phone.

Now, Heather was being sly enough about it—her eyes were on the board while her thumbs were flying around under the desk—but still, it was dangerous.

So I started thinking that maybe what she was upset about was something bigger than having five "losers" on her Love Connection list.

Maybe it was something real.

I was dying to talk to Marissa about it during drama, but she didn't show up to class. She hadn't said anything about leaving school early, so I asked a couple of people if they knew where she was but got nowhere. Then Billy came up to me and whispered, "Pay-phone Casey the minute school lets out. He says it's important."

"Did he say anything else?"

He shook his head.

"Wait. When which school lets out? Ours or his?"

"Ours."

"But he'll still be in class!"

He shrugged. "I don't decipher, I just deliver."

He turned to go, but I grabbed him and said, "Do you know why Marissa's not in class?"

He looked around. "She's not?"

"Mr. Pratt!" Mr. Chester hollered at him. "How many times do I have to ask you to stay on task?"

"Sorry, sir!" Billy called back, and hurried off to the scenery he was supposed to be painting.

I really wanted to chase after Billy and ask him more, but I was pretty sure he didn't know any more. And then I noticed Heather lurking to the side of the stage and started wondering if maybe *she* did. She was still sneaking texts, and I could tell this wasn't just casual conversation.

She was *plotting* something.

And after Billy's message I started getting the sinking feeling that what she was plotting involved Casey.

And probably me.

TWO

The minute school let out I hurried over to the pay phone. It wasn't like I had to rush so I'd get to it before someone else did, since everyone else on the planet has a cell phone. But after watching Heather's texting get more and more intense during drama, and then having her singe me with her infamous Psycho Evil Eye as she bolted out of the classroom, I was dying to know what was going on.

"Hey, it's me," I said when I heard Casey answer.

"You okay?"

He sounded stressed, which made me look around for Heather. "Yeah. . . . What's going on?"

"Heather didn't say anything?"

"She fried me with an evil eye, but that's all. What's this about?"

I could hear him take a deep breath, then let it out in a long, puffy stream. "Your mom and my dad."

For a split second I panicked.

Were they in an accident?

Were they *dead*?

Apparently Casey can read minds, because he says, "They're fine." Then he adds, "But it looks like they're getting married this weekend."

"What?"

"In Vegas."

I yanked my jaw off the ground. "How do you know? Did your dad tell you?" But before he can answer, I get totally ticked off. "This is so typical! Of course she wouldn't tell me! Of course she has to go off and be secretive and sneaky and not even think about how this is going to mess with my life!"

"If it makes you feel any better, my dad didn't tell me, either."

"She's a *horrible* influence on him!" Then I add, "But then . . . how do you know?"

"I overheard my mom talking to Heather about how she'd hired a private investigator."

It takes a minute for that to really sink in. "You're serious? Why'd she do *that*?"

He sighs. "She thinks he should be paying more child support than he is."

"So she hired a private investigator? To find out *what*?"

"I don't know. You know how she is."

"And he found out they're getting *married*?"

"He found out that my dad made a 'sizable purchase' at a jewelry store yesterday and bought two plane tickets to Las Vegas."

"For today?"

"Yup."

"But we don't *know* they're getting married."

"It sure points that way, don't you think?"

I let *that* sink in, too, then sigh. "Yeah, it does."

"I tried confronting my mom, but she went into a tirade about eavesdropping and then accused me of still seeing you."

"What did you say?"

"Well, you know I can't admit it."

I sigh. "I know."

"So since she told me the usual nothing, I've been trying to reach my dad, but his cell's been turned off all day. You can try your mom, but I'll bet you won't get through."

"You think they've already left?"

"Yeah. And phones off is their Do Not Disturb sign."

All of a sudden I'm just *mad*. "She hasn't even told me who my real dad is, and now she's sneaking off to marry *your* dad?"

"My dad's not a bad guy, if that's any consolation."

"Well, your stepmom-to-be is going to take care of that! He's already becoming just like her!"

He gives a little snort. "So true."

"I wonder if Grams knows."

"Would she tell you?"

"She may be good at keeping my mom's secrets, but I can't believe she'd keep *this* from me!"

"Okay. Well, if she tells you anything, can you let me know?"

"Via Billy?"

"Yeah."

Then I ask, "So what's your mom doing about it? Anything?"

"What *can* she do?"

"Fly to Vegas and cause a scene?"

He laughs. "She might if it would change things. But they're divorced, so that would be pretty over-the-top, don't you think?"

We're both quiet, and then he says, "Sorry for the bad news."

I hesitate but finally say what I'm thinking. "Is it going to weird you out too much?"

"Just don't start calling me your stepbrother."

I pinch my eyes closed. "I hate her."

"Why don't you find out if your grandmother knows anything." Then he adds, "And, Sammy?"

I choke out, "Yeah?" because I'm on the verge of crying. I mean, why couldn't I have a normal mom and a normal life? Why did things have to be so complicated and full of all this stupid *drama*.

And then Casey says something that pushes me over the edge. "I love you."

"I love you, too," I tell him in a really stupid blubbery way.

He laughs. "And don't worry. Nothing's going to change that." Then he says, "Keep me posted," and gets off the phone.

I was probably madder at my mom than I'd ever been, and believe me, that's saying something. So my skateboard ride home was fast and furious, and even though

I was careful like I always am when I sneak up the fire escape and into Grams' apartment, there was *steam* coming off of me.

Now, the thing about living illegally in a place where the walls are paper-thin and the neighbors are nosy is that you can't go yelling or demanding or banging around.

You have to be *q-u-i-e-t,* even when you're steaming mad.

"Grams?" I whispered, dumping my skateboard and backpack.

No answer.

"Grams!" I snapped—in a hoarse, kinda whispery steaming-mad way.

No answer.

I checked around the apartment, and since there's only one bedroom and one bathroom, it was quick.

No Grams.

No Grams, and no note.

Now, okay. Normally I meet up with Casey at the graveyard after school or hang out with my friends a little or, you know, get sidetracked on my way home. So yeah, I was home really early—so early that Grams would probably have been shocked to see me. But still. Her *not* being here seemed weird to me, and I couldn't help wondering . . . *did* she know my mom was getting married? And if so, how long had she known?

Wait. Maybe she had gone to stop her.

Maybe she was on her way to Las Vegas right now!

Or . . . maybe she was going to be the maid of honor!

Or, you know, the *old maid* of honor.

Whatever!

But . . . she wouldn't do that to me! If she were on her way to Vegas, it would be to put a stop to the wedding, not to be in it!

So there I am, in the kitchen, convincing myself that Grams wouldn't go anywhere without at least leaving a note and a massive list of dos and don'ts, when all of a sudden the phone rings.

"Aaah!" I choke out as I jump about ten feet in the air. Then I just stand there, looking at the phone ringing off the hook, wondering if it's Grams calling me from Vegas, or maybe my mother calling to confess that she's eloping, or maybe Casey calling with an update.

Living in an ancient, run-down highrise with an old wall phone and no caller ID is no fun, believe me.

Anyway, I finally stuff my heart back down my throat and pick up the phone. "Hello?" I warble in my best old lady imitation.

"Is Sammy there? It's Marissa."

"Marissa!" I drop the old lady act quick. "Are you okay? Where were you during sixth period?"

"My life is *such* a mess," she says.

"Tell me about it!" But she's obviously really desperate about something, so I don't say anything about my mom eloping with Casey's dad. I just ask, "What happened?"

"My dad again, of course. Mom's dragging me to Vegas. We're getting ready to drop Mikey off at Hudson's, then we're going to the airport!"

To make a long story short, Hudson Graham is the

coolest old guy you'd ever want to meet, and his house has become a safe haven for Marissa and her brother, Mikey, when their parents are in extreme crisis mode—which has been often lately.

Still.

This was extra extreme.

"Now?" I ask her. "But why is she taking *you*?"

"She thinks me begging Dad to stop ruining our lives at the blackjack table might shock him into seeing how his gambling is hurting everyone in the family." She sighs. "But he already knows, and I really, really don't want to go."

"So don't go."

"She's making me!" She takes a deep breath and says, "Anyway, I won't be at the dance tomorrow, just so you know."

I wanted to laugh and say, Well, at least you don't have to worry about Rudy asking you to dance, but before I could, another thought booted that one right out of my brain. A thought that made me gasp. Made me feel light-headed.

Like any second I might fall over.

Or float away.

Her voice was in my ear but seemed miles away. "Look, I've got to go. Wish me luck."

"Luck," I whispered.

After she hung up, I tried my mother's cell number.

Sure enough, a mechanical voice told me she was "unavailable."

I hung up and stood there, trying to remember how to breathe.

Trying to stop thinking what I was thinking.

It was crazy.

I knew it was crazy.

Unfortunately, that's never stopped me before.

THREE

I did leave Grams a note.

I had trouble figuring out what to say, because Grams is a big worrier and this was actually something she *should* be worried about. If she didn't already know about my mom's latest stunt, I didn't want to write anything that would make her go crazy, but I also didn't want her to stop me. So I wound up writing *Gone until—? Don't worry. I'll call!*

Then I grabbed my repacked backpack and my skateboard and tore out of there.

It's hard to plan things out if you don't know *how* to do something. And the truth is, I was clueless. So instead of thinking about the big picture, I focused on taking things one step at a time. Chances were really good that I wasn't going to get past Step One anyway, so even if I could have thought things through to the end, it didn't seem like I should waste time trying. Besides, Step One was so extreme that I couldn't even think about Step Two, let alone how I'd make it to The End.

Now, usually when I ride my skateboard fast, it helps calm me down. Helps clear my mind. But this time it didn't help at all. I tore past the mall, down Cook Street to Cypress, and the way my heart was pounding had nothing to do with going ninety miles an hour on a skateboard. And then it practically exploded when I saw Mrs. McKenze's car parked in front of Hudson's house.

Step One was still a possibility.

I did not want to go up to the house. Hudson may be seventy-three, but he's one of my most trusted friends, and he'd for sure figure out that I was up to something. And since he and Grams have gotten really close, telling him anything would be like pulling the plug before the faucet was even turned on.

Luckily, Marissa was sitting in the car, alone. She opened the passenger door when she saw me coming. "Hey! What are you doing here?"

"Shh!" I told her and dived in the backseat next to two small suitcases in the spot where Mikey must have been sitting.

"What are you doing?"

I crammed my skateboard out of sight and twisted out of my backpack. "Coming with you."

"What? To *Vegas*?"

"My mom's eloping with Casey's dad."

"No!" She squints at me. "Ew."

"Exactly. Plus, I'm royally ticked. She still hasn't told me who my father is and she thinks she can up and marry my boyfriend's dad? I am done taking this. And if she hates me forever for busting in on her wedding, I don't care!"

"But . . . Sammy, we're not driving, we're *flying*."

"I know. I've got my reward money. I just need a ride to the airport. And maybe an adult to, you know, look like I'm with?"

She does a nervous glance out the window toward the house. "Do you have your birth certificate or . . . some kind of ID?"

I blink at her. "I have my school ID."

"That's not gonna get you on an airplane!"

"It's not? Well . . . what do you use?"

"I . . . I don't know! My mom gets the tickets, and I always just go with her."

"No ID?"

She shakes her head.

"So, see? No problem."

"But . . . she buys the tickets ahead of time! We've already got our boarding passes!" She rummages through her mom's purse and finds two slips of paper. "We're on American, flight two forty-six."

I had no idea how any of it worked, but I didn't want Marissa giving me away when her mom returned, so I just tried to sound like I knew what I was doing. "Look, it'll be fine. I'm just gonna stow away until we get to the airport, then you distract her while I slip out and get a ticket for that same flight."

"It would be awesome if you could come, but I—" Then she sees her mom hurrying down the steps and gasps, "Hide!" as she rips off her sweatshirt and throws it over my head.

Mrs. McKenze drives a kinda sporty Lexus, so even though there isn't much room to hide, I squoosh down behind the driver's seat and bite back an *Ow!* when Marissa dumps a suitcase on top of me.

Then the driver's door opens and Mrs. McKenze gets in. "Thank God for Hudson," she says as she fires up the car.

And before I can finish thinking that this is the craziest, *stupidest* idea I've ever had, she's got the car in gear and we're zooming away.

The ride over to the airport was weird.

Quiet.

And—even contorted and buried, I could tell—heavy with tension.

At one point Marissa said, "Mom?" but Mrs. McKenze just snapped, "Not now. I'm thinking."

And that's all they said until we nose-dived to a stop in the airport parking lot and Mrs. McKenze said, "We're barely going to make it."

"Mom?"

"Get the luggage."

So while Mrs. McKenze puts up the dash protector and gets the windows adjusted, Marissa hustles around and opens the back door.

I crawl out onto the pavement and scurry around behind the car. Marissa's eyes are all bugged out as she passes me my skateboard and backpack and mouths, "Unbelievable!" Then she pulls out the suitcases in time for her mom to beep the locks shut and say, "Let's go!"

I peek around the car and watch them run to the terminal, and when enough time has passed, I get on my skateboard and fly across the parking lot.

The Santa Martina airport is not LAX or JFK or some other big place where I've heard you can get swallowed up or lost or tangled up in big security mazes.

It's got one door, one counter, and one security line.

And the planes that fly out of it are nothing but puddle jumpers.

Seriously, I think they double as crop dusters.

Anyway, I spot Marissa and her mom in the security line putting stuff into bins, and Marissa spots me, too, and gives me a quick nod as I hustle up to the counter.

"Yes?" the woman behind the counter asks.

She has big plastic earmuffs looped around her neck and is wearing a bright orange vest that has her airport ID dangling from it.

"I'm hoping to catch flight two forty-six to Las Vegas." I nod over at Marissa. "My cousin and aunt invited me last minute."

The woman behind the counter looks over to the security line, and since Marissa's watching me, I give her a happy wave and she waves back.

"How old are you?"

"Thirteen," I tell her, then slip my school ID across the counter and hold my breath.

She doesn't ask for a birth certificate. She doesn't pull a face or, you know, *scrutinize* me. She just ticky-types at a computer keyboard and nods. "I do have a seat. How will you be paying?"

"Cash," I tell her, and pull out my wad of reward money.

"Checking luggage?"

"Pardon me?"

"Are you checking luggage? Or do you only have carry-on?"

"Uh . . . carry-on?"

She looks over the counter at my stuff. "That should be okay."

So I pay for my ticket, and after a little more ticky-typing, she hands me a slip of thick paper and says, "Here's your boarding pass. Get through security right away. They've already begun boarding."

Marissa and her mom have disappeared through the security station, and since there's no line, I just go up to the guy in uniform and hand him my boarding pass.

"Shoes off," he tells me. "Sweatshirt off. Bag through the X-ray. Skateboard, too. You wearing a belt? Wait. You got a computer in there?"

I'm scrambling around like crazy trying to follow his instructions, and by the time I've made it through the security arch, I'm half undressed and feeling really disjointed and dorky.

I grab my stuff as it comes through the X-ray machine but don't see Marissa or her mom anywhere. And since a guy standing by a door that leads outside is saying, "We've got one more," into a walkie-talkie, I'm feeling really frazzled and like I don't have time to put on my shoes.

"It's okay," he tells me as I go stumbling toward him

with my shoes dangling. He takes the boarding pass from between my teeth, tears a part off, and hands the little part back. "They'll wait."

So I sit down right there on the floor and wrestle into my high-tops, then grab my stuff and race out the door and down the ramp.

There are two little planes on the tarmac, but only one has steps going up to it. Steps that were rolled right up to the plane's open doorway. A woman in a blue uniform leans out of the doorway and waves me along. "Las Vegas?" she calls.

So I rush over and pound up the stairs, and when I'm inside, she gives me a sunny smile and says, "Welcome aboard."

"Thanks," I pant.

Her name tag says NELLY, and she eyes my skateboard. "I'm not sure that will fit in the overhead. They're small." She reaches for it and smiles. "How about I keep it up front?"

So I turn my skateboard over to her and say, "Where should I sit?"

"Your first flight?" she asks, and when I nod, she smiles and points to 7A on my boarding pass. "Just follow the seat numbers along the overhead compartments."

So I turn the corner, and right away I spot Marissa and her mother in the second row.

Now, this plane is three seats across. A is the window seat on the right side of the aisle, and B and C are two seats on the left side of the aisle.

And since there are only about twelve rows, it would be totally impossible to get on board without Mrs. McKenze seeing me.

Which is fine.

I need her to see me.

How else am I going to get from the airport to . . . the wedding chapel or . . . or wherever it is I'm going?

Which all of a sudden hits me is Step Three of a plan I didn't really believe would get past Step One.

"Samantha?" Mrs. McKenze says as I go down the aisle.

"Mrs. McKenze?" I ask, dropping my jaw. I laugh. *"Marissa?"*

Marissa shakes her head and looks at me all bug-eyed as she mouths, "Unbelievable!"

Mrs. McKenze is still not clicking into the reality of me being there. "You're alone?"

I nod. "I'm going to meet my mother in Las Vegas." Then I hurry past them to 7A, and after I've shoved my backpack under the seat and buckled up like Nelly instructs over the speaker system, the propellers fire up.

My heart starts slamming around even harder as we roll forward. Out my window I can see the woman who'd sold me my ticket. She's on the pavement outside with her ear-muffs on, directing traffic—or at least our plane—with big orange wands, motioning us forward and then sideways until we're on the runway. Then she hustles away and out of view.

We rumble along for a while, and then we stop and idle. And after a few minutes of just sitting there, I'm thinking, Uh-oh. I'm busted. They're going to turn the plane around and kick me off.

And part of my brain's going, No, no, no! Just keep going. *Fly*.

But another part of me is going, Yes, yes, yes! Kick me off!

I mean, what am I *thinking*?

What am I *doing*?

My brain is such a complete mess that I'm even having trouble remembering what my mission is.

I know I'm mad at my mom, but . . . what good is going to Las Vegas?

Lady Lana always does what she wants anyway.

And then we lurch forward and my head slams back into the headrest, and as the plane roars down the runway, rattling and shaking like it's about to come apart at the seams, I close my eyes and hold on for dear life.

There's no turning back now.

FOUR

Mrs. McKenze is not my biggest fan. I don't know *exactly* why, but I think it has something to do with a certain unauthorized trip Marissa and I took to Hollywood to see my mom.

Or maybe it was that incident where we almost got killed by a creepy gang guy in a basement in Tigertown.

Or it could be because of the time Marissa and I started out for a school dance in a limo but ended up at the golf course with the arm of a corpse.

After that one, Mrs. McKenze told Marissa she should "reassess the wisdom" of her friendship with me, but I think her problem with me actually started way back with that trip to Hollywood.

Which all of a sudden seems kinda ironic, seeing how here we are, on another wild trip because of my mother.

Well, at least that's why *I'm* here.

Anyway, after we're up in the air, I look out the window again, this time trying to get my bearings. I'm feeling a strange mixture of excitement and terror. It's awesome to be up in the air, but at first we're tilting side to side, which is scary because the whole plane feels really unsteady. Like either the pilot's new or we're gonna crash.

Maybe both.

And after we finally quit seesawing around, we start banking. I'm talking *way* over to the side, so when I look out my window, I'm practically looking straight down.

Nelly's not coming on the intercom screaming, *Mayday! Mayday!* or anything, but I'm death-gripping my armrests because the airplane is making such a loud roar and rumble that I'm sure it's just gonna shake apart.

We do finally level off, but my heart's still pounding and we're still rumbling and I'm thinking that my seat cushion—which Nelly had announced could be used as a "flotation device"—would be a lot more useful if it were a parachute. I mean, what good is a stupid flotation device when you're nowhere near water? You can bet the pilot isn't relying on his stupid seat cushion to save his life. He probably has a parachute at the ready! Why does he get one when all we get is a stupid cushion?

And then someone taps me on the shoulder.

I jump and turn, but it's not the pilot handing over his parachute.

It's Nelly handing out little packs of blue foam earplugs. "Thanks!" I call, and she smiles and nods, then moves on.

The earplugs help a lot. They cut the roar of the plane, and somehow also make it so I can sort of hear what the people in 7B and 7C are saying to each other. In a weird way they also make me feel safer. Like not being able to *hear* the noise that makes it seem like the plane's about to fall apart means the plane might actually *not* fall apart.

Which doesn't make sense, but still, it helps.

The funny thing about flying over an area you know well is realizing that you don't know it at all. I'm looking out the window going, Where's the mall? Where's our school? Where's the Senior Highrise? trying to distract myself from shaking apart without a parachute, but I don't recognize anything.

And then after we've leveled off, we start flying over empty land and little mountains and I can see a lake off in the distance.

A lake?

There's no lake near Santa Martina!

Is there?

And if that *is* a lake, why aren't we flying *over* it so I can use my crummy little cushion in case we crash?

All of a sudden someone shoves my arm, and when I jump and turn again, it's still not the pilot with his parachute.

It's Marissa, with blue plugs poking out of her ears, squatting in the aisle, her eyes darting back to her mother up in 2B. "I can't believe you actually got on board!" She's whispering, but what's funny is I can hear her fine.

"I know, huh?" I whisper back.

"So now what?"

I shake my head. "I have no idea!"

"Well, where's your mother staying?"

"I don't know!"

She stares at me. "You don't *know*?" She collects herself a bit and says, "So you're going to call her when we land?"

I pull a little face. "She's turned her cell phone off. So has Casey's dad."

Her eyes are bugging. "Sammy, Las Vegas is *huge*. How are you planning to find her?"

"I figured I'd look up wedding chapels?"

"But—"

"*And,*" I say, trying to sound optimistic, "you know the Elvis impersonator who used to work at Maynard's Market? He's moved to Vegas and he told me I should look him up if I was ever in town. He might be able to help."

She starts wagging her head so fast it looks like *it's* about to shake loose. "Sammy! There have got to be a hundred Elvis impersonators in Las Vegas. Maybe two hundred! How are you ever going to know which one he is?"

"He told me his name?"

That seems to shock her because our Elvis never, ever went out of character. "He did?"

"Yeah. It's Pete Decker."

"Did he give you a phone number?"

"No."

She holds both sides of her head like she's trying to keep it from bursting open.

"*But* I've also got this!" I say, digging up my backpack and pulling out an oversized postcard with pictures of my mom on it. There's a headshot, a full-length shot, and one of her as Jewel, the character she played on *The Lords of Willow Heights*.

Marissa turns the card over and speed-reads the back, which lists a bunch of information about my mom, her credits, and how to contact her. "She has an agent? *And* management?"

I shrug. "Yeah. I didn't know that either."

"Where'd you get this?"

"Grams had it. Mom gave her a few and I snagged one on my way out the door. I thought it might help me find her."

She hands it back and just shakes her head. "You really have no idea what you're doing, do you?"

I look down. "It all happened really fast, okay?"

"I hate to break it to you, but you will never in a million years find her."

Just then Nelly's voice comes over the intercom. "The aisle needs to remain clear at all times."

We look toward the front of the plane and there's Nelly, holding her telephone, staring right at us. And then Mrs. McKenze cranes around and gives Marissa a stern look.

"Uh-oh, gotta go," Marissa says, and for the rest of the trip she stays up in 2C while I stare out the 7A window, watching the sky get dimmer and dimmer as I try to convince myself that finding my mother won't be impossible.

I know there's a lot of stuff about Las Vegas on TV, but I don't watch much TV, so most of what I knew about Vegas came from Marissa. The McKenzes have gone there a lot, which, looking back on it, was probably because Mr. McKenze wanted to go. Marissa always made Vegas sound like it was fun, and it probably is if you've got tons of money like the McKenzes used to. She would go on and on about the resort pools and the shopping and the shows.

It seemed like a great place. But after it came out that Mr. McKenze had a serious gambling problem and had wiped them out financially, Marissa started talking about Vegas like it was the devil's playground.

My first clue that we were almost there was when Nelly gave us a bunch of instructions about getting ready for landing. My seat and tray table were in the same position as when I'd gotten on board, and I didn't have any electronic devices that needed shutting off, so I went back to staring out the window.

It was dark outside, and there hadn't been much to see for a while, but now I'm noticing a green glow in the distance. It's like a giant brilliant emerald poking up out of the desert.

As we get closer, I can see other lights. *Miles* of lights. And as we go down, down, down toward the runway, I can hear the people across the aisle from me going, "Look! There's the Luxor! And there's Mandalay Bay!" like they're spotting celebrities.

And then we're bumping onto the ground and fishtailing a little before Nelly comes on the intercom and says, "What do we say, gang?"

I'm thinking she means we should all say, "Thank you for not crashing!" but instead a bunch of people on the plane shout, "Whoa, Nelly!"

Regulars, I guess.

Anyway, she laughs, "Exactly!" then adds, "Welcome to Las Vegas!" and gives us instructions that basically boil down to Don't Get Up Until I Tell You To.

So I sit there buckled in and try to fight the feeling of

panic that's washing over me. I mean, what's Step Three? It's dark, and I have no idea where I'm going or staying or even how much hotels cost.

And I need to save enough money to get back to Santa Martina.

All of a sudden I just want to stay buckled in and go straight back home.

What am I *doing*?

When we're finally let off the plane, I get my skateboard back from Nelly and follow the passengers in front of me into the airport terminal—a big circular building with lots of windows and slot machines.

Slot machines.

At the *airport*.

Like you could gamble first thing, or last thing, depending on if you were coming or going.

The McKenzes are ahead of me, rolling along their suitcases, and Marissa's sort of lagging behind her mom, who's talking on her cell phone. I catch up to her quick, and she whispers, "I told my mom I didn't want to leave until I was sure your mom was here."

"But my mom's not coming!" I whisper back.

"I know! But your mom's got a reputation for being flaky, right? So I'm thinking we'll say that she's flaked again. We can't leave you here!" She looks ahead, keeping an eye on her mother. "I told her you'd never been here and had never flown before and were kind of a basket case because your mom's marrying your boyfriend's dad."

My eyes pop. "You told her all that?"

"What else was I supposed to say? Sammy, you being here is *crazy*."

"Sorry. No. You did great. And thank you for not just leaving me here."

She snorts. "Believe me, you do not want to be thirteen and alone in Las Vegas. Especially if you're a girl."

Mrs. McKenze is about ten steps in front of us and so intent on talking on her phone that she hasn't even noticed that Marissa's dropped back to walk with me. I take a deep breath. "So what did your mom say about what you told her?"

"She thinks your mom's a selfish diva."

"Really? Wow." I hesitate. "And here I thought *I* was the one she didn't like."

Marissa eyes me like, Well, yeah. There's that, too. Then she says, "But she's got bigger things to worry about than your bad influence."

"So what's *her* plan? Where's your dad?"

Just then we hear Mrs. McKenze cry, "He's *what*?" She staggers to the nearest chair and falls into it like a rag doll. Her hand's shaking like mad as she holds it over her eyes. "Was it Leon?"

"Uh-oh," I whisper to Marissa as we stand by watching her mother shaking, because this is sounding really bad.

Like maybe he's *dead*.

"Leon's his favorite dealer," Marissa whispers back, like that explains everything.

"What's it called?" Mrs. McKenze asks, rummaging around in her purse for something to write with. She scribbles on a scrap of paper and says, "I have no idea how to do that."

We just hold our breath, waiting and watching while Mrs. McKenze listens for the longest time. And while she's listening, I try to decipher what she's scribbled on the scrap of paper. It looks like *Clark Co Det Cntr,* which I figure is Clark Company Det-something Center, but I haven't figured out what the Det-something is yet when Mrs. McKenze gets off the phone.

"What is it, Mom?" Marissa asks. "Is Dad all right?"

Mrs. McKenze is panting. Hyperventilating. "That was the security manager at the casino." She pinches her eyes closed. "Your father," she finally says, "is in jail."

FIVE

"Jail?" Marissa gasps. "What did he do?"

Now, the McKenzes have always been really hush-hush about their personal problems. Marissa's not *allowed* to talk about them, and I do understand that . . . kind of. But it's not just that Marissa's parents don't want her bagging on the family like a lot of kids at school do with theirs. It's that they have an *image* to uphold. They want to be seen as "successful investors."

From what I've been able to figure out, a "successful investor" makes money investing other people's money. In what, I'm not sure, but I think the stock market's a big part of it, because all the McKenzes' problems started when their stock investments took a nosedive. And I guess if you're playing with other people's money, you don't really want them to know that you've got financial problems yourself—especially not a gambling problem.

So where Mr. and Mrs. McKenze used to just project success—you know, with their cars and their mansion and the way they dress and act and all of that—since their finances went in the toilet, they've also become super secretive. And even though I know that Mrs. McKenze has been tearing her hair out for months over her husband's gambling, she still always *acts* like nothing's wrong. She drives the same car and dresses the same way and talks like everything is just dandy.

But inside the mansion, dishes have been flying.

Anyway, the point is, she would never let on to me that her world was falling apart, and according to the McKenze Code of Honor, Marissa should never have made a peep about it to me or anyone else.

So when Marissa says, "Jail?" I can see the tired wheels in her mother's brain calculate the damage as she looks from her daughter to me and back again. And I can tell she's trying to devise some cover-up reason why her husband could possibly be in jail, only the wheels won't turn.

She's just done.

"Mom?" Marissa finally prompts. "Why's Dad in jail?" Then she adds, "Sammy knows about the gambling," which makes Mrs. McKenze put a hand up to her forehead like she can't believe Marissa did such a stupid thing. So Marissa tells her, "Look, I had to talk to somebody—living with you and Dad has been a nightmare!"

Mrs. McKenze closes her eyes and nods. "I know." She gives a sad little shrug. "And I'm afraid things are beyond repair at this point."

"What happened?" Marissa asks, sliding into the chair beside her.

Mrs. McKenze looks at me and sighs. "I hope you can be a good friend to Marissa and keep this between us."

I nod and Marissa says, "Sammy's like a vault, Mom. You know that."

Her mom takes a deep breath, holds it for forever, and finally says, "He punched Leon in the face. Broke his nose."

"He punched *Leon*? But . . . he always talks about Leon like he's his best bud."

"Well, your father was—and probably still is—drunk."

Marissa shakes her head. "But still, he *punched* him? *Why?*"

"Because your father came to town with a big bundle of cash and lost it all at Leon's blackjack table."

"How much money are we talking about?"

"A lot."

"But . . . where'd he get the money? I thought everything had been cut off."

Mrs. McKenze studies her for the longest time, and finally she says, "He got it from his brother."

"Uncle Bruce?" Marissa gasps, and when Mrs. McKenze nods, I understand right away that this has become bigger than a gambling problem.

This has become a hole so dark and deep that there is no getting out of it.

See, Marissa's family may have been rich, but Marissa's uncle is richer. And Marissa has told me that it's not just that her uncle has more money than her dad, it's also that her uncle is an eye surgeon. And since he's on local commercials and billboards promoting his "world-renowned vision center," he's become kind of a celebrity in Santa Martina. People around town see him and whisper, "Hey, isn't that the guy on the billboard?" And when Marissa's

39

dad meets new people, more and more he gets asked, "Say, are you related to Dr. McKenze?"

And as Dr. McKenze's world-renowned vision center became at least *county*-renowned, he got richer and now lives in a place that makes the McKenzes' mansion look like a tract house.

Which all of a sudden hit me was maybe the reason Mr. McKenze started gambling in the first place. How else was he going to keep up?

Anyway, after Marissa gasps, "Uncle Bruce?" she follows up with "Why in the world did he lend Dad money?" but I'm pretty sure I know the answer.

He didn't know his brother had a gambling problem.

"You'll have to ask your father how he managed that," Mrs. McKenze says as she collects her things and stands up, and I can tell she's thinking she's already said too much.

"Wait, so what are we going to do? Bail Dad out of jail?"

"I'm not sure how to go about doing any of this." She frowns. "But I'm sure Sammy's mother is wondering what's taking her so long, so we should get going." And after we've walked for a ways, she asks me, "Is she meeting you in baggage claim?"

"Uh . . . I didn't check any luggage."

She looks me up and down. "Aren't you in the wedding? Don't you have a dress?" Then before I can figure out how to wiggle out of *that* one, she decides the answer for herself. "Oh, she's probably doing one of those rental packages."

I nod. "I don't really know what the plan is."

"I'm surprised your grandmother isn't here with you." She eyes me. "I wouldn't send Marissa to Las Vegas alone."

And since there are obvious holes in my story, I try to change the subject before she asks me any more questions. "I'm really sorry about your problems. I wish there was something I could do to help."

She sort of shakes her head. "I wish there was, too."

Then we walk—actually, more like march—through the airport, past glitzy shops and restaurants and slot machines.

Loads and loads of slot machines.

And when we get down to the bottom of an escalator, Mrs. McKenze looks around and says, "Well, this is baggage claim. I'd think your mother would be waiting for you here."

So we follow her past these big metal luggage carousels, which are mostly just sitting there empty, to one that's going around and has luggage on it. "This is the one for our flight," she says, looking at the people hanging near the area. "Do you see her?"

I walk to the other side of the carousel, checking here and there and all around, and finally I come back and shake my head. "I don't see her."

"Hmm. Well, the two of you wait here for her while I take care of the car rental." She points across the building. "I'll be right over there." Then she gives Marissa a stern look and says, "Do not go anywhere until I get back!"

The minute she's gone, Marissa says, "This is insane! What are you planning to do here? How are you going to get around? You don't even know where your mother's staying or where they're getting married or anything? And my dad's in jail. Jail! If my mom finds out your mom isn't coming and that you just jumped on a plane, she is going to kill me."

"You? Why you?"

She tilts her head. "*How* did you get to the airport? *Who's* going along with your crazy scheme? Sammy, there's no way she's going to believe I didn't know anything about this."

"So we've just got to find my mother."

"We?"

I shrug and look down.

"Sammy! My dad is in jail, do you get that? We're having a family crisis! I can't excuse myself from it to find your ditzy mother!"

"I know, I know."

"So what's your plan? What are we supposed to do with you?"

"Nothing. I'll be fine."

She rolls her eyes.

"Look. I have money. I'll just get a room."

"What if they won't rent you a room? What if you need a credit card in case of damages?"

"What?"

"You know—like you throw the television out the window or rip up the couch."

"What?"

"People do that, you know."

"Why?"

"'Cause they think they're rock stars. 'Cause they're stupid."

"Well, I'm not a rock star and I'm not stupid."

"But they don't *know* that."

"Look at me!"

She eyes my ripped jeans and high-tops. "You could pass for a rock star. Some of them dress like that."

"I'm thirteen!"

"Exactly! And nobody's going to rent a room to a thirteen-year-old rock star. You would totally destroy the place."

"I'm not a rock star!"

She shrugs. "They don't know that."

I throw my hands in the air. "Good grief."

So instead of talking about things that maybe could have helped the situation, Marissa and I argued about dumb stuff like that, and then all of a sudden Mrs. McKenze is back and our time is up.

"Maybe she's outside?" Mrs. McKenze asks, and she's looking pretty frantic.

So we go to a pickup area outside big glass doors, and after I've pretended to scour the sidewalk and streets for my mother, I ask Mrs. McKenze, "Could I use your phone to call her?"

"Sure," she says, and it's easy to see that she'd really like to move this along.

So I dial my mom's cell phone, and when I get the "unavailable" message, I click off and hand the phone back. "Her phone's off."

"It's *off*?"

I nod.

"Well . . ." She looks around. "What are we going to do?"

"I'll just wait for her here," I say with a shrug. "I'll be fine."

"No, you won't!" Marissa says, then turns to her mom. "We can't just leave her here."

Mrs. McKenze scratches the back of her head. "Your mother's probably just running late, right, Sammy?"

I look down and shrug again. "I'm sure that's it."

She studies me a minute. "Well, she wouldn't *not* pick you up, right?"

I keep on looking down 'cause I'm feeling pretty bad about working her toward what's obviously become Step Three. I mean, I can't just let her *leave* me here. But instead of confessing what I've done and begging for mercy, I tell her, "Just go ahead. You've already got enough to worry about. I'll be fine."

She looks at her watch, then checks all around trying to figure out what to do. "Are you *sure*?" she finally asks.

"No!" Marissa cries. "There's no way we're leaving her here!"

So we wait around another ten minutes searching for my phantom mom, trying her phone again, shaking our heads, until finally Mrs. McKenze asks, "What hotel is your mother staying at?"

And I'm about to say I don't know, but Marissa scoots behind her mother and mouths something big and exaggerated at me.

"Uh . . . ," I tell Mrs. McKenze as I try to figure out what Marissa's saying, "I think it starts with an *M*."

Marissa nods like crazy, then does her big, exaggerated mouthing thing again, but I'm still not getting it.

"Mandalay Bay?" Mrs. McKenze asks.

Marissa shakes her head and air-paints the letters *M-G-M*.

"Uh, no," I tell Mrs. McKenze. "I think it was . . ." And then I just go for it. "Is there a hotel called MGM?"

Mrs. McKenze's eyebrows go flying. "You're staying at the MGM Grand? That's where we're staying!"

Marissa steps forward. "How about we give Sammy a ride over and figure things out from there?" She looks at me. "Your mother must have checked in by now, right?"

The instant I nod, Mrs. McKenze grabs her stuff and says, "Well, come on then, let's go." And as she heads off to a moving walkway across the street, I take a deep, choppy breath and tell Marissa, "Thanks."

Then right away I start wondering how in the world we're going to pull off Step Four.

SIX

By the time we'd taken a shuttle bus to the car rental lot and were driving into town, it was seven-thirty, but it didn't *seem* like nighttime because everything was lit up, including the nonstop billboards for concerts and fights and comedians and "illusionists" and "peep shows" . . . all blazing with lights and flashing parts.

"How much were tickets to that show?" I ask Marissa as I point out the billboard for Darren Cole and the Troublemakers, 'cause his "Waiting for Rain to Fall" is Casey's and my song, and Marissa had told me that her family had seen him in concert during one of their pre-crisis trips to Las Vegas.

Darren Cole is no kid, and people like Candi Acosta swoon over him, so I try not to think too much about the fact that "our" song is done by an old guy, or that Candi Acosta also likes it, because thinking about that is just . . . gross.

But there was the billboard, and I found myself asking anyway.

And missing Casey.

"Mom?" Marissa asks. "Were they expensive?"

"Were what, huh?"

"The Darren Cole tickets." Then she adds, "Sammy's a fan."

"I'm not a *fan*," I tell her, but it doesn't matter. Mrs. McKenze is already giving me a buttery look in the rear-view mirror.

"Worth every penny," she sighs.

Which didn't answer my question, but it's not like I had time to go check out Darren Cole anyway. I had a mother to find!

Marissa points to a billboard with blazing blue faces. "They were good, too," she says, then points to the next one. "So was he! . . . And so were they!"

Mrs. McKenze says, "We have seen a lot of shows, haven't we?" She shakes her head and mutters, "And now we get to see the jail."

What a roller-coaster life the McKenzes were having. And the truth is, I used to be jealous of everything they had. Not that I'd ever wanted their *life*—Marissa and Mikey were basically orphaned by their parents' jobs, left on their own in their mansion like ignored pets—but all the *stuff*? The *vacations*? When everything you own fits inside one little drawer, and you've been a whole lot of no-where for vacation, watching your best friend living large can get pretty discouraging.

And hearing about it can get kind of annoying.

But now here they were, shooting down the tracks, trapped inside a cart of gigantic debt, holding on for dear life as they blasted their way toward jail.

Anyway, while I'm taking a little mental ride on the

McKenzes' roller coaster, wondering if a loop-the-loop was ahead for them or if jail was the end of the ride, Mrs. McKenze misses a driveway and lets out a little curse. And then when traffic pins her in so she has to turn right, she lets out a bigger curse and says, "I do *not* want to be on the Strip!"

"This is the Strip?" I ask, leaning forward between the seats.

"And it's Friday night of a three-day weekend," she moans when she sees all the traffic. "We are just stuck."

When we turn onto the Strip—which the road sign says is actually Las Vegas Boulevard—all I can do is gawk. The emerald building I had seen from the air is on our right, and it's *huge*. Huge and glowing, with an enormous gold lion in front.

"That's where we're staying," Marissa says, pointing to the green building.

"It is?" I gasp.

"That's the MGM lion."

All of a sudden I make a connection. "The one that roars in movies?"

"That's it!" Then she adds, "Well, not *that* one, but you know." Then she points across the street to a giant Statue of Liberty standing in front of a hotel that has an *actual* roller coaster going all around it. With people riding it! "That's New York–New York," she says, then points behind us. "That castle? That's Excalibur. And the pyramid next to it? That's the Luxor. And that big gold building even farther down is Mandalay Bay. It has an awesome beach."

"A *beach?*"

"Uh-huh. With a gigantic wave pool. It's like being on Maui!"

"It's nothing like being on Maui," Mrs. McKenze grumbles. "And there are never enough loungers."

I look up and down the Strip and say, "I can't believe all the *lights*," and it comes out kind of gaspy because, really, I can't believe all the lights!

"No energy crisis here," Mrs. McKenze says. "In the summer they keep the casinos at sixty-five . . . and they leave the doors open! So you burn up on the Strip, then freeze to death inside." She slams on the brakes and practically hits the car in front of us. "I hate this place," she mutters.

So she may be hating it, but I'm just awestruck, soaking in all the buildings and lights and *people*. I've never seen so many people on sidewalks. They're packed together and just moseying, but even so they're going faster than we are.

"Here," Mrs. McKenze says, handing over her phone. "Try your mother again."

So I do, and when I get the "unavailable" message, I hand the phone back and say, "I wonder if her phone's broken or something."

"I have never understood her," Mrs. McKenze says. "She has always been . . . aloof."

"Aloof?"

She eyes me. "How about we call it 'distant.' I tried to connect with her at school functions when you two were little, but she always seemed like she was . . . elsewhere. It was hard to carry on a conversation." She shrugs. "Maybe it was the age difference. She was a young mom. The rest of us were . . . older."

I give a little snort. "Nah. She's still that way."

"Well, at least she's realized her dream." She glances back at me. "Being on *Lords* is a big deal."

"Uh . . . *was*, I guess."

"What do you mean?"

"It's been canceled."

She whips around to actually look at me. "*Lords* has?"

"Uh-huh."

She grips the wheel tighter. "Wow. That's the end of an era, huh?"

"I guess."

"I used to watch it when I was in my teens and twenties. I used to *record* it because I didn't want to miss a thing."

Marissa stares at her. "Really?"

She tosses a smile at Marissa. "Then I had you and Mikey, and that was the end of the luxury of my soaps!" She looks at me in the mirror. "So what is she going to do now? Does she have something else lined up?"

"For her next act," I say, sounding all peppy, "she's going to marry my boyfriend's father!"

Mrs. McKenze pulls a little face, and I can tell she's biting her tongue.

Biting it hard.

It takes us at least half an hour to circle the block and get into the MGM Grand's parking structure. And once the car's locked up and we've collected all our stuff, we go down an elevator and then walk through ground-level parking to some big glass doors that lead into a wide tunnel of shops. At the end of the shops there's an escalator, and when we get to the top of that, we turn the corner and wind up in the biggest hotel lobby I've ever seen.

Actually, the only other hotel lobby I've been in is the Heavenly Hotel's, right across the street from the Senior Highrise. It's got ancient furniture and heavy curtains and threadbare carpet. . . . It's so old it might actually be kind of cool if it wasn't for the smell. The place stinks like moldy potatoes.

Or maybe rat pee.

Hmm. Now that I think about it, probably both.

Plus, when you sneeze inside the Heavenly's lobby, you send up clouds of dust, which, of course, make you sneeze some more. So once you start sneezing, you can get a whole dust storm going. Seriously. It creates an atmospheric *event*. I'm surprised it's never made the Weather Channel.

But *anyway,* the MGM lobby is nothing like the Heavenly's. It's more a huge glistening ballroom with chandeliers and gold sparkling everywhere. On our right there's a mile-long check-in counter with a whole wall of screens behind it. On our left are shops with lots of glass walls and gold accents, and in the middle is a flower arrangement the size of Grams' apartment.

"Impressive, huh?" Marissa says, 'cause my jaw is dangling.

"I can't afford to stay here!" I whisper.

"It's actually pretty cheap," she whispers back. "But

don't worry. I'll get you in our room. Just go up like you're checking in, then tell my mom your mom hasn't arrived yet."

"I don't even know *how* to check in! What am I supposed to do?"

"Just go up and act like your mom's supposed to be here. I'll keep my mom back. Trust me. This will work."

There are about twenty check-in lines, so I stand in the one next to Marissa and her mother like I know what I'm doing. And when I get up to the front of the line, I smile at the lady across the counter and say, "I'm meeting my mom here. Her last name is Keyes. Has she checked in already?"

Her fingers fly across her keyboard. *"K-E-Y-S?"* she asks.

"K-E-Y-E-S," I tell her. I try to sound calm, but my mouth is dry and I'm feeling really stupid acting like my mom's here when I know she's not.

"Could it be under a different name?"

"Uh, Acosta?" I tell her, just putting out another lie. *"A-C-O-S-T-A."*

She ticky-types some more, then says, "Oh, here it is. Two guests?"

The rest of me feels stun-gunned, but my head manages to bob up and down.

"She hasn't arrived yet." She checks me over. "And we'll need a credit card and photo ID, so I'm afraid you'll just have to wait until she's here."

My head bobs some more and I manage to choke out,

"Thanks," as I back away from the counter and hurry over to Marissa.

"Well?" Marissa's mom asks, because they still haven't made it to the front of their line.

"She hasn't arrived yet." I try to sound confident, but I'm feeling really light-headed. Like any minute I might just keel over.

It's Mrs. McKenze's turn now, so she goes up to the counter while Marissa hangs back with me and says, "You look really pale."

"She's here," I whisper.

"She *is*?"

"Well, she will be. The reservation's under 'Acosta'— for two people."

Marissa gasps. "There's a wedding chapel right inside this hotel!"

"There is?"

"Yes! You pass by it on the way to the Lazy River."

"The Lazy River?"

"The pool!" She points. "It's that way. Through the casino, past the food court . . . I bet they're getting married right here!" She shakes her head. "I cannot believe it. She could have stayed any one of a million places, and she's staying right here?"

I just stand there blinking like an idiot.

She laughs, then says, "*You're* the one who should take up gambling. Nobody gets this lucky."

It did seem incredibly lucky. And maybe for once it was my turn to have a little luck, but I'm not used to it, so it felt more like a mirage than something real. Like any moment, *poof,* it would disappear.

I tried not to question why I was having good luck instead of bad. I just tried to think about what my next step should be.

And what in the world I would say to my mother.

SEVEN

It didn't seem to faze Mrs. McKenze much when she found out that my mom hadn't checked in yet. "Just come with us," she said, marching across the shiny marble floor. "You two can keep each other company while I figure out what I'm going to do."

Marissa gave me a little thumbs-up and a grin, but I was too busy with the knot in my stomach to appreciate that we'd just pulled off Step Four.

Which was weird.

I mean, here I'd escaped my grandmother, stowed away in a car, jumped a plane to Las Vegas, weaseled my way into Mrs. McKenze's hotel room . . . and I was freaking out about seeing my mother?

I guess that tells you something about my mother. Don't get me wrong—it's not like I was worried about her raging at me.

Lady Lana raging?

Please.

But I *was* there to mess up her wedding. Or at least that's what would happen when I appeared out of nowhere and raged at *her*. Because you know what? I'd had enough. If she didn't tell me who my dad was, I wasn't going to let her marry me a stepdad—*especially* not my boyfriend's father—without a fight.

And somehow getting ready for that battle scared me more than anything else I'd done so far. I mean, hadn't I ruined her life enough? Hadn't my just being alive gotten in the way of . . . everything? She'd almost *died* once trying to cover up that I was her daughter, because she thought it made her seem too old for a part she was auditioning to get. And she'd almost married some guy who had no clue I existed, because he was a Hollywood hotshot who was crazy over her and she felt like she had to. And when I'd asked her if she loved the guy, she'd frowned and said, "We can see how far *love's* gotten me."

So yeah. I've felt like a burden for a long, long time. And the only consolation—the only actual *clue* I'd gotten—was that whoever my dad was, she *had* been in love with him at one point.

So me being alive wasn't my *fault*.

Still. My brain was good at finding ways to forget that.

It was also good at wondering if I wasn't jumping to wrong conclusions. Maybe she'd just *said* that bit about being in love to protect me from the truth. Maybe my father was actually a violent criminal. A horrible, heinous man, and just the sight of me reminded her of the terror she'd gone through.

Or maybe he was a weirdo who'd kidnapped her

and held her on some remote property in the redwoods. Maybe he'd brainwashed her into *believing* she was in love with him. Maybe she'd left me with Grams so she could escape her past. Escape the memories. Escape what I represented.

But then what was his catcher's mitt doing in Grams' closet?

So maybe she'd run away to a commune to escape Grams and her rules. Maybe the commune held big softball tournaments with other communes, and she'd fallen in love with the catcher from another commune and had joined it to be with him!

And that's how my brain runs off to the Land of Maybe and gets hopelessly lost. I can never seem to find my way out, and it's *exhausting* being in there. I've spent so many nights wandering through dark alleys and down dead ends in the Land of Maybe that I'm just sick of it. I don't want to go there anymore.

But the only way out is through answers.

Real answers.

And that's what I was going to get.

So as we marched along behind Mrs. McKenze, I decided that once my mother was checked in, Step Five was going to be to park at her door and not let her leave until she told me the truth.

Even if that meant pinning her down and mussing up her fancy wedding dress.

Mrs. McKenze had obviously stayed at the MGM before, because she led us out of the giant lobby toward a carpeted area with slot machines and then took a sharp right down a wide hallway without even slowing down. The place was packed, so Marissa and I had to dodge and weave around people just to keep up.

Near the end of the hallway, we passed by a little convenience store and entered a sort of walking roundabout with a huge tiered water feature in the middle of it. The roundabout had a bunch of hallways coming off it, and Mrs. McKenze made a beeline for one that led us to a bank of elevators.

Now, okay, it *was* Friday night of a long weekend in Las Vegas, but good grief, there were people everywhere. People with drinks, people with luggage, people decked out in rhinestones, people in swim cover-ups and flip-flops . . . And they were all *going* someplace. I felt like a lost little minnow in a river of salmon that were all swimming in different directions.

"Come on!" Mrs. McKenze called from inside an elevator. The thing was already completely full, and there was no way Marissa and her stuff and me and my backpack and skateboard were going to fit. But Mrs. McKenze gave us a fierce look and held the door, so we said, "Sorry! Sorry!" and squeezed inside.

We got off at the fourteenth floor and started down a hallway that was, like, two hundred feet long. I didn't know how far we were going, but I was really tempted to throw down my skateboard. "It would be way faster to ride," I whispered to Marissa.

"That would be very rock 'n' roll of you," she said.

"Don't you dare go rock 'n' roll on me!" Mrs. McKenze

said over her shoulder. "I don't need more problems than I already have!"

She was sounding kinda frantic, so I held on to my board and told her, "Don't worry, I have no plans to go rock 'n' roll on you. And I'll make sure Marissa doesn't, either."

"No TVs out the window, Mom, promise," Marissa said with a laugh.

Mrs. McKenze's head just wobbled. Like, Please, Lord, save me. But when it turned out our room was the very last one on the right, Marissa and I eyed each other.

It would have been way faster to ride!

Anyway, the room was big. It had a bedroom with its own sitting area, a living room with a huge couch and two cushy chairs, a kitchen area, and a huge bathroom. It was three times as big as Grams' apartment.

"You're serious?" I whispered to Marissa, 'cause I'd never been in any place like it.

But Marissa sighed and shook her head like this was a miserable excuse for a hotel room. "We used to get a deluxe suite. . . . You should have seen it."

"Well, that couch looks pretty comfortable to me," I whispered, and it did. A lot more comfortable than Grams' couch.

And that's when it hits me.

Grams!

"Uh . . ." I look around. "I need to find a way to call Grams."

Marissa hesitates. "Does she know . . . anything?"

"I left her a note, but it just said I didn't know when

I'd be home and that I'd call." I spot a digital clock next to the couch. "That was five hours ago!"

"So what are you going to tell her?"

Just then Mrs. McKenze comes out of the bedroom scrolling through her cell phone as she says, "I've got to make some calls, so please just give me a few uninterrupted minutes," and before we can say a thing, she's closed the bedroom door tight.

"Quick," Marissa says, "do it now!" She hands me the room phone and punches in Grams' number, and as it's ringing, she whispers, "Good thing you guys don't have caller ID."

But the truth is, I'm not sure if I care if Grams knows where I am anymore. I mean, it depends. If she knows Mom's getting married, then I'm furious with her, too. But if this is another case of Lady Lana not caring how what she does affects me *or* Grams, then I don't want Grams to worry about me being in Las Vegas.

All of a sudden there's no time to think about it. "Hello?" Grams says on the other end.

"Hi, Grams, it's me. Sorry I couldn't get to a phone sooner."

"Where *are* you?"

"I'm with Marissa."

She hesitates, then hrmphs and says, "We all know what *that* can mean."

"What are you saying?"

"You know exactly what I'm saying."

She was leading me down a sidetrack where I didn't

want to go, so I brought it back to the reason I'd called. "Well, I just wanted to let you know I'm fine, and that I'm spending the night with Marissa."

I can practically see her eyebrows go flying. "You're telling me, not asking me?"

I take a deep breath. "Marissa's all stressed out about her dad, so please? I promise you, I'm safe, and Marissa's mother is here, so you have nothing to worry about." And since she's not arguing and it feels like I may have miraculously worked this conversation so I won't have to tell her where I am, I decide it doesn't matter at this point if she already knows what my mother is up to. "So . . . I'll talk to you tomorrow, okay?"

"Wait!" she says, and I can tell her granny radar has kicked in. Probably because she can tell I'm trying to get off the phone. "Are you at their house? Why did it take this long for you to call me?"

My brain races around for an answer and finally I tell her, "This was the first chance I had to call."

"So where are you?"

"With Marissa and her mom." And because I know that's not going to cut it, I add, "In a hotel."

"In a hotel? Where?" And then, like a crack starting across a sheet of ice, she asks, "What if your mother calls wanting to . . . wanting to talk to you?"

I can feel myself drifting away from her. "When's the last time she's done *that*?"

"Samantha! Why aren't you telling me where you are?"

"Maybe because you didn't tell me about Mom's little weekend getaway?"

It comes out cold.

Hard.

There's a moment of silence and then I can feel her start to panic. "Samantha . . . Samantha, please tell me you're not in Las Vegas."

And just like that, my whole body is shaking, chattering away.

She knew!

"But I'm not supposed to lie to you, remember?" I tell her through my teeth.

"Samantha!" she wails, but I'm totally iced over. Her being upset just slides right off me. She knew! After everything my mom's put her through, she's still willing to keep her secrets. Still choosing her over me. "Sorry, Grams, but I'm done listening to you stick up for Mom. Her getting married is stupid and selfish and *mean,* and I'm done just taking this."

"Her getting—"

"I didn't want *you* to worry about where I was, but since you've known about this all along, I don't know why I even cared!"

"Samantha—"

"Maybe if *you'd* stood up to her sooner, I wouldn't have to sneak into cars and hop onto planes and weasel my way into other people's hotel rooms!"

"Samantha, please—"

"*No!* I'm done!" I shout. "I can't believe you kept this

from me!" Then I slam down the phone and burst into tears.

"Wow," Marissa says, putting an arm around me. "Are you okay?"

"No!" I shout at her. "I'm not okay! Grams knew! She *knew*."

Marissa looks over her shoulder at her mother's bedroom door and tells me, "Shhh!"

"Sorry," I mumble, but I just feel so . . . betrayed.

"What in the *world* is going on?" Mrs. McKenze cries, flinging her door open.

"I'm sorry," I whimper. "I'm really, really sorry."

And I'm not thinking about anything but being betrayed, but apparently Marissa is. "Would it be okay if Sammy slept on the couch tonight?"

"Slept on the . . ." Mrs. McKenze moves in closer. "What happened?"

Marissa heaves a sigh. "Her mother." Then she shakes her head a little, like, Don't even ask.

So Mrs. McKenze takes a deep breath and says, "It's fine. And, Marissa, sweetheart, I've got to fill out forms online for your father—getting him out is not going to be as easy as I'd hoped."

"Why?"

"Because we have to post bail, and I don't know if I do that at the justice court or the district court—I don't even know the difference! And I can't talk to your father, because inmates are not allowed to receive calls." She holds her head like it might explode. "Inmates! Your father is an inmate!" She lets go and says, "And we can't visit him without filling out forms . . . but first I have to register, and I'm not sure how or where to do that." She shakes her head and whimpers, "I feel like Sammy—I just want to cry. And I have *such* a headache." She gives Marissa a pleading look. "Could you two go down to that little store by the water fountain and get me some aspirin and maybe get us all some sandwiches? We completely missed dinner."

As upset as I was about Grams, I knew I was also just *hungry.* And I guess Marissa was, too, because she grabs me by the arm and yanks me off the couch and says, "Sure."

"Promise me you'll stick together, okay?" She hands Marissa some cash. "And please come right back."

So off we go, down the corridor to the elevators, down the elevators to the water fountain, and past the water fountain to the convenience store. And since Marissa is either blocking it out or in denial about her dad being in jail, she keeps asking me what I'm going to do instead of talking about what she's going through.

And the truth is, I'm kind of glad, because it feels good to just walk and talk with Marissa and plan out how I'm going to confront my mother. Marissa even makes me laugh a couple of times, which helps a lot. And we do exactly what Mrs. McKenze asked us to—we buy the aspirin and sandwiches and head straight back.

Which, if you ask anybody, qualifies as a minor miracle.

On our way back up we're the first people on the elevator, which I discover is actually worse than being the last. People keep cramming on and we keep squooshing back. And just as we're sure the elevator can't fit any more

people, we hear a voice cry, "Hold the door," and someone actually does.

And then in squeezes a woman with a huge red suitcase.

Marissa grabs onto me and gasps, and like a ton of turds
it hits me.

My luck had been just a mirage.

EIGHT

I turn away from the elevator door and duck while people squoosh in tighter. Marissa stoops, too, and we look at each other all bug-eyed as we hear, "Excuse me . . . excuse me . . . oh, thank you . . . I'm sorry . . . we're getting off at four . . . can you . . . ? Thank you."

Then the door closes.

I don't dare look as the elevator goes up, but I'm pretty sure I know who the other half of "we" is. Then the elevator stops, and I hear her voice go, "This is it, Mom," and I know I'm right.

"What are *they* doing here?" Marissa mouths.

I'm just working out that the reservation for Acosta must not be for Warren and my mom, but for Warren's ex and the last person on earth I want to deal with—Heather.

But them being in Las Vegas actually does make sense. "Probably the same thing I am," I whisper to Marissa.

Marissa shakes her head. "Wow. Your mother has no idea what she's in for."

The doors are open, and since Heather and Candi are

already off the elevator and there's no time to *think*, I grab Marissa and announce, "Excuse us, we have to get off here, too," and push forward.

"No!" Marissa whispers, yanking back.

I drag her along. "Yes!"

The fourth floor looks just like the fourteenth, with a short elevator hallway that leads to an open area with a bunch of long corridors branching off it like the spokes of a wheel. Heather and her mother are already out of sight, so I hurry toward the open area and catch a glimpse of a big red suitcase disappearing down a corridor to our right. "There they go!"

But Marissa stays put by the elevators.

"Come on!" I whisper, waving her along.

She finally takes a few steps forward. "Why? I don't want to talk to them! And I promised Mom we'd be right back! What are you going to do if my mother gets mad and kicks you out?"

I move forward so I can peek down the corridor. "I just want to see where they're staying, okay? Nothing else."

She finally gives in and we watch as Heather and her mother stop at a door about a third of the way down the corridor and slide their card in about six different ways before unlocking it and going inside.

Since the doors down the corridor all look the same, it would be easy to lose track of which room they went into, but there's a tray with dishes outside the room right across the hall from them. So I've got my mark, and the second Heather and Candi's door closes, I jet down, read the room number, and jet back. "Four fifty-six," I pant when I join up with Marissa.

"So now what?"

"Now we get back to your mom!"

Once we're on the fourteenth floor and don't have to worry about people in the elevator hearing, Marissa says, "So if they're here and your mom's *not,* how are you ever going to find her?"

I don't have an answer, so I just march along saying a whole lot of nothing.

"Well, do you think *Heather* knows where they're staying? They wouldn't have come clear out here if they didn't know more than we do, right?"

We're practically running down the hallway to make up for my little detour, and it's hard to run *and* think *and* be in shock. "I don't know! But she's sure not going to tell me!"

"So true." Then when we get to the door, she whispers, "So do you want to look up wedding chapels and start calling around?"

"*Now?*"

"I think a lot of them are open all night."

So the minute Mrs. McKenze's disappeared back inside her room with the aspirin and a sandwich, we dive into our food as we dig through the room's phone book. And almost right away we discover that there are about a hundred wedding chapels in Las Vegas.

"You've got to be kidding," I say through a mouthful. "It'll take us all night to call these!"

"And what if they didn't make an appointment? Some people just show up, wait in line, and get married."

I shake my head. "I'm never going to find her."

"You're just now getting that?" Then she rubs it in by pointing to an ad that reads, Love in the Fast Lane— Drive-Thru Weddings. "I doubt people get appointments for that." She points to another ad, for the Love Me Tender Wedding Chapel that has a picture of a white gazebo with Elvis playing an acoustic guitar. "Can you see your mom getting married by Elvis?"

"No! I can't see my mom doing any of this stuff! I can't even believe she'd get married here! It's so tacky!"

Marissa takes a huge bite of her sandwich but still manages to say, "She's never had a wedding, right? So maybe because you and your grandmother are against her marrying Casey's dad, this is the closest she can get to a dream wedding."

"Getting married in Las Vegas is not even *close* to a dream wedding!"

Marissa shrugs. "Maybe getting married here has just been stigmatized."

"Stigmatized? *Stigmatized?*"

"Sure. Here, look at this," she says, pointing to another ad. "This one offers limousine transportation, a fresh floral bouquet, professional photographs. . . . And the wedding parties I've seen at the chapel downstairs are always decked out." She shrugs. "They look classy."

"Classy," I say, staring at her like she's lost her very last marble.

She gets up and goes to the sink for a glass of water. "I'm just saying, if there are a hundred chapels, not *all* of them are going to be tacky!"

"Well, great," I say, getting up for a glass of my own. "If there are a hundred potentially untacky chapels, how will I ever find the one she's going to? And since my mom's *not* staying at this hotel after all, how will I ever find her?"

"That's what I've been saying this whole time!"

"I didn't know there were a hundred chapels! That changes everything!"

For a while we both focus on eating instead of talking. And then Marissa tosses her sandwich wrapper in the trash and says, "Maybe you should call and ask your grandmother?"

"No! And she wouldn't tell me anyway. She's weird about my mother." I toss my wrapper, too. "I think she's afraid of her."

"She's . . . but why? Your mother may be full of herself, but she's not someone I'd be *afraid* of."

I think about this a minute and then kind of shake my head. "It's more like she's afraid of her reaction to things. Maybe when you don't have much family, you're afraid to lose what you do have?"

We sit around some more, and finally Marissa grabs the phone book and says, "Well, let's start at the top and work our way down."

"You're serious?"

"You got a better idea?"

Just then Mrs. McKenze comes out of the bedroom and says, "The CCDC is open until midnight."

Marissa looks up. "The CCDC?"

"Listen to me," Mrs. McKenze mutters. "I sound like a

pro." She takes a deep breath and says, "The Clark County Detention Center, also known as the jail."

"Oh."

"And I won't be able to visit or even talk to your father"—she looks at her pad of paper—"also known as inmate zero-one-zero-seven-two-nine-zero-one . . . until we go down to the CCDC in person to register."

"But when's he getting out?" Marissa asks.

"I don't think that's going to happen tonight." She checks her notes. "We can post bail until midnight, but I don't think they'll just release him. I think there's a whole procedure they follow."

"How far away is the jail?"

"Only a few miles." She looks back at her notes. "On South Casino Center Boulevard."

Marissa mutters, "How appropriate."

Mrs. McKenze turns to me. "So I'm sorry, Sammy, but we have to go. You're welcome to stay here, but honestly, I can't take on worrying about you. I've got too much to deal with as it is."

"I'll be fine," I tell her. "I really appreciate you letting me stay here."

She grabs her blazer and purse. "Someday I want to hear about your mother, but not now."

Marissa follows her mom toward the door, but at the last minute she runs back and slips me her room key. "If you want more than that lousy sandwich, there's a McDonald's downstairs in the food court. Pizza, too. Just turn right at the fountain, and then stay to the right. You'll run into it. Everywhere else is super expensive."

Mrs. McKenze is holding the door, waiting. "Marissa, let's go!"

"Coming!" Marissa calls over to her mom, then whispers, "Good luck!"

"You too!" I whisper back. "And thank you!" And really, I can't believe how helpful and *nice* Marissa's been. Especially considering her dad's in *jail*.

And then they're gone.

And it's really quiet.

And for some reason I just sit there, alone in that big hotel room with green glowing lights outside and complete silence inside. And the longer I sit there, the smaller I feel.

The *stupider* I feel.

What was I thinking?

Then fear starts creeping in. It's a panicky, spidery feeling that tells me I'm trapped.

Helpless.

And if there's one thing I can't stand, it's feeling helpless.

So I grab the pen and pad by the phone, put the phone book in my lap, and start trying to track down my mother.

Now, during the first few calls I was nervous and kinda stuttery. For one thing, the fact that they even answered the phone surprised me. I was *glad* they did, but it was late and the idea that you could get married at this hour still seemed . . . bizarre.

So was having the phone answered by Elvis. I mean, it's really hard to get out what you need to ask when the person on the other end is going, "Viva Las Vegas, baby!"

and making stupid Elvis jokes like "Will you be hitchin' up your hound dog t'night?"

But after about the tenth wedding chapel, I got the hang of it and just said the same thing, over and over: "Hi, I'm wondering if this is the chapel where Lana Keyes and Warren Acosta will be getting married—it's either tomorrow or Sunday. I flew in last minute and forgot my invitation."

And at every single one I got the same basic answer—sorry, not here.

After almost an hour of this I still had miles of numbers to call. And since it *had* been a lousy sandwich and I *was* hungry, and there was no way I was going to get through the whole list of chapels before Marissa's mom got back anyway, I was just talking myself into going down to the food court when I got an idea.

It was a stupid idea, but at that point any idea seemed better than calling another chapel. So I went with the stupid idea.

I dialed 411 and answered the recorded voice with "Las Vegas . . . Peter Decker."

A live person came on and said, "I have two. A 'Peter L.' and an 'Elvis Enterprises.'"

My heart started pounding. "The Elvis one."

"Here it is," she said, and clicked over to a computerized voice.

I scribbled down the number, then hung up and just sat there holding my breath, wondering if it was crazy to call, especially since it was late and I had no idea what I wanted to ask or how he could help me.

But I felt at a total dead end, and the thought of calling the rest of the chapels seemed worse than making one senseless phone call to Elvis.

So I dialed.

And on the fourth ring I heard, "You've reached the King. Leave me your name and number and I'll get back atcha as soon as I'm havin' a little less conversation. Or if you want to do the Jailhouse Rock, my cell number is—"

I scribbled down the digits he rattled off and before I could talk myself out of it, I dialed his cell.

After the second ring a husky voice says, "You've reached the King."

I go, "Pete?" but it sort of sticks in my throat, so I try again, louder. "Pete Decker? It's Sammy."

I can hear a bunch of noise in the background. Cars. People. Horns. Music.

And then the King says, "From Santa Martina?"

"Yes!" And all of a sudden I'm stupidly happy.

"Hey, little mama!" he says, and he sounds stupidly happy, too. "Are you in Vegas?"

"Yeah."

He hesitates. "Are you callin' for tickets? 'Cause I don't have a show yet—I'm just workin' the Strip."

"Actually, no, I'm looking for somebody, and I'm wondering if maybe you have connections to wedding chapels."

"Wedding chapels?"

"Yeah. The person I'm looking for is getting married this weekend."

"Hang on," he says, and then he's gone for, like, two

minutes before he says, "Thank you . . . thank you very much," to someone and gets back on the phone. "Sorry," he says in his regular voice. "Photo op." Then he goes, "Hang on," again, and two minutes later he's finally back, saying, "Look, I'm workin', and Elvis with a cell phone is just *tacky*. You think maybe you can come down here?"

"Uh . . . where are you?"

"Across the street from the Bellagio."

"What's the Bellagio?"

"A resort on the Strip. Near Caesars Palace?"

"How far is it from the MGM Grand?"

"It's not bad. I'm just past Paris Las Vegas." I hear someone call, "Hey, Elvis!" and then he says, "I gotta go," and hangs up.

So I scribble a note that says, *I'll be back soon,* then I grab my backpack and skateboard and Marissa's room key and jet out of there.

NINE

I find myself wandering through the casino as I try to get out of the hotel and onto the Strip, and let me tell you, it feels pretty dicey. I mean, I've got a backpack and a skateboard and I'm wearing ragged jeans and trashed high-tops, and there's no way anyone's going to mistake me for an adult. Plus it's not like there are other teenagers in the casino. Everyone else is way older, and even the ones who *aren't* dressed up are dressed way better than I am.

But there I am, walking between banks of slot machines, past big green gambling tables with dealers and cocktail waitresses and people just hanging around, and nobody says, Hey! What's that kid doing in here?

It's like I'm invisible.

Which I guess is a good thing, but still. Something about it makes me feel . . . strange. Like I could get into serious trouble and no one would care.

Or know.

Or even *notice*.

Anyway, I don't actually know where I'm going and I'm afraid to ask. So the whole time I'm walking, I'm nervous, but in a sort of conflicted way. Part of me's afraid that someone's going to kidnap me and no one will care, and part of me's afraid that a casino guard will grab me and lock me up until they track down some adult who's willing to claim me.

Good luck there.

Anyway, with my eyes darting around for kidnappers and casino guards, it takes me a while to notice that there are signs with arrows hanging from the ceiling that tell you which way to go for what. And when I spot one that says Las Vegas Blvd. thataway, I go thataway until I find the next sign and the next, and finally I see big glass doors that lead outside.

So just getting out of the MGM is like escaping a little city. And then after asking somebody which direction the Bellagio is, I'm still not able to get *moving*, because I'm stuck in a herd of humans. Seriously, it's like a cattle drive on the sidewalk. It's a *wide* sidewalk, too, but there's no way I can ride my skateboard. Besides all the pedestrians moseying along, the flow's being plugged up by people handing out brochures or hawking helicopter rides over Hoover Dam and the Grand Canyon.

Now, the Hoover Dam and Grand Canyon people just holler at you, trying to get you to sign up for a ride. It's the people handing out pamphlets that are like annoying gnats, buzzing around everywhere. They all do this same slapping thing with their little pamphlets. Slap-slap-slap, they flick their stack against their hand, then step in your way and shove one at you.

The first time one got forced on me and I saw that it had pictures of mostly naked women, I dropped it like a nuked potato.

The next time, I shoved it back and snapped, "I'm thirteen, you idiot! You think I'm going to call your stupid Hot Women hotline?"

He either didn't hear me through his earbuds or didn't speak English, because he just went back to slap-slap-slapping his stack and turned to the next person coming his way.

Anyway, the farther I walk, the more it seems like the Strip doesn't know what it wants to be. For example, there's a store that has fifty-foot M&M's characters looming above the sidewalk. They're like Godzilla M&M's ready to jump down and crush everyone on the sidewalk.

But still.

They're M&M's.

Sweet, innocent, yummy candy.

There are also costumed characters like SpongeBob and Patrick who wave at people going by. And people with jewelry carts or in little tiki huts selling sunglasses. And all the lights everywhere are *amazing* and make you feel like you're in some fantasy kingdom.

But in between the M&M's and SpongeBobs and sunglasses are rowdy bars and Pamphlet People and bums with signs that say WHY LIE? I NEED A BEER. Plus wasted musicians with open instrument cases begging for change. And delivery trucks rolling by with skanky pictures of women painted on them. Stuff that makes you remember, Oh yeah, I'm in Sin City. Still. It may be getting close to midnight in Sin

City, but there are so many people and so many lights that the seedy things aren't making me *scared,* just cautious.

Now, the lady I'd asked for directions had told me that the giant lit-up *O* down the Strip was the Bellagio, and since I can now see that, plus a big sign for Caesars Palace, I'm definitely going the right way. But what's weird is that I keep walking and walking and walking . . . and walking and walking and walking . . . but I don't seem to be getting any closer to the big *O* or the Caesars Palace sign. It's like I'm walking on a giant cement treadmill going past the same Pamphlet People over and over, getting nowhere.

Which I guess is because everything is so oversized that even though it looks like it's right *there,* it's not. And when someone tells you that something's on the next block, what that really means is that it's a mile away, because the blocks go on *forever.*

Anyway, I finally make it to a fake Eiffel Tower and a big lit-up hot air balloon that has PARIS written in the middle of it, so I know I'm getting close. And then, as the sidewalk sort of swoops to the right, I spot Elvis.

My heart does a little Wa-hoo! But then I see that there are actually three Elvises.

Whoa, wait—and a Mini-Elvis.

Mini-Elvis is definitely not a kid, but he is . . . little. I stand off to the side and watch for a while as people go up and have their picture taken with an Elvis, then slip him some money and continue on down the Strip. The Elvises are all wearing some variation on the same white-and-gold Elvis costume, with bell-bottom pants and a wide gold belt, and they've all got the black Elvis hair and muttonchops and sunglasses. The Mini-Elvis isn't getting any takers, and the other three seem to be annoyed that he's there and keep their distance from him. But I guess no one owns the corner, because Mini-E stays in the game, calling out, "Come on, baby! Let me be your teddy bear!" to women as they walk by.

Anyway, at first I'm not sure which one of the Elvises is Pete. I know it's not Mini-Elvis, and I know it's not the luxury-sized Elvis, but either of the other two could be him.

Or neither could be.

So I just stand there watching, until finally one of the midsized Elvises does a double take at me, then tosses me a grin and a wink. "Hey, little mama!"

I nod at him, but I'm still not a hundred percent sure it's Pete until he comes across the walkway and says, "You're not here alone, are you?"

Now, what's sort of weird for me about all this is that when Pete worked nights at Maynard's Market, he was always Elvis. Everything he said was an Elvis phrase or song title. Half the time I couldn't figure out the meaning of what he was saying, because pretty much the only thing I know about Elvis Presley is from Pete working the counter at Maynard's.

Anyway, him talking to me now in his regular voice is not something I'm used to. And I'm actually thinking, Are you *my* Elvis? when he says, "Sammy, you should probably not be cruising the Strip alone on a Friday night. I wouldn't even suggest it on a Sunday morning, 'cause some of these cats prowl clear through to dawn." He lifts one of his Elvis eyebrows. "I don't care how tough you *think* you are, nobody your size is tough enough."

"I'm only here because . . ." And all of a sudden I feel really stupid.

Why did I think an Elvis impersonator could help me?

"Because . . . ?" he asks.

I shake my head and look down. "It's a long story."

"Sammy, I don't have *time* for a long story. But . . . tell me you're not in Vegas alone. How'd you get here?"

I give a little shrug. "Part of the long story."

"But . . . *why* are you here? Can't you give me the CliffsNotes?"

I take a deep breath and say, "My mom's getting married to my boyfriend's father in Vegas this weekend."

"Ouch," he says, pulling a face. Then he raises that Elvis eyebrow again and says, "Who knew who first?"

"I knew my boyfriend *way* first."

"Dirty pool," he says with a tisk.

"*And* she won't tell me who my dad is."

This sinks in a minute, then he says, "You have no idea? Why won't she tell you?"

I shake my head. "She won't tell me that, either." Then I add, "She's a diva." I swing off my pack and pull out the big card with her pictures on it. "Her name's Lana Keyes, and she plays Jewel in *The Lords of Willow Heights*."

"That's your *mama*?" he gasps, taking the card.

"Yeah," I grumble. "A little-known fact that she's mostly embarrassed about."

"Whoa," he says, and now both his Elvis eyebrows are reaching for his big black pouf of hair.

"Please don't tell me you watch *Lords*."

"As long as you don't tell anyone I do!" he says with a laugh.

I shake my head. "Unbelievable."

"But addicting!" Now I see a little mental shift happen under his pouffy 'do as he checks out both sides of the photo card. "If ambition's a dream with a V-8 engine, she sure is revvin' hers."

"Huh?"

He zooms in on me. "She has you sneakin' in and out of the Highrise while she's livin' large as Jewel?" He snorts. "That's just wrong."

And now I'm seeing that this was a bad idea.

A *very* bad idea.

"Uh . . . who told you that?"

"Nobody. I just pieced it together." He eyes me through his shades. "And don't worry. Elvis always plays it close to the vest."

That didn't make me feel a whole lot better.

Actually, I felt worse.

All this time I thought I'd been so stealthy, and *Elvis* had figured it out?

"Look, Sammy," he says. "Don't worry about that. The more I think about this, the more I don't like your situation. Or that you're here. Especially that you're here alone." He studies me. "So how can I help you?"

"I don't know," I tell him, taking the card back. "It was probably stupid. I thought maybe you had some kind of connection with the wedding chapels. You know—since Elvises marry people around here? And I thought you

82

might be able to contact them for me to see if my mom's getting married at any of them. There's a hundred chapels in this stupid city, and I called, like, a third of them tonight and got nowhere."

"So the mission is to stop the wedding?"

I nod, then kind of take it back. "Mostly I'm here to find out who my dad is. And if she won't tell me, then, yeah, I'm gonna be a major monkey wrench in her wedding party."

He thinks a minute, then says, "Her name's Lana Keyes and his is . . . ?"

"Warren Acosta."

"Acosta?"

"Right."

He takes a picture of the picture of my mom with his phone and says, "Since she's a diva, she won't be tyin' the knot in some second-class chapel, right?"

I nod 'cause that sure seems right to me. "But I couldn't really tell the difference from the phone book. Some have big ads but—"

He shakes his head like, No-no-no, then says, "I got this. What's your cell number?"

"I don't have one."

"What?"

I shrug. "Yeah, I know. Stupid."

"Well, how am I supposed to reach you?"

"Can I call you?"

"Sure." He frowns. "But not every ten minutes! And what if we have a sighting?"

"A sighting?"

"Of your mother!"

"Oh."

He shakes his head. "This is no good. I need a number."

"I'm at the MGM. In room fourteen eighty."

He raises an eyebrow. "So you're gonna be hangin' around a hotel room waitin' on a call? I think I know you better'n that."

"Well . . . can I get back to you with a number? I'll figure something out."

"Sure, sure, no problem," he says, stepping away. "I'll do what I can, but right now I've got to get back to work if I'm gonna make rent." He gives me one last eyebrow lift as he goes back to full-on Elvis. "Take good care and be safe, little mama."

"Thanks," I call, then head up the Strip.

It was after midnight when I got back to the hotel room, and the minute I came through the door, Marissa pounced. "Where have you been?"

"Getting food!" I said, showing her what was left of the pizza slice that I'd bought on the way back. "Didn't you get my note?"

She eyes me suspiciously. "I'm not your grandmother, you know. Why'd you take all your stuff?" Then her eyes pop. "Don't tell me you rode your skateboard around the hotel!"

I grin at her and say, "Much quicker than walking," but now I'm closer and can tell she's been crying. So I put down my stuff and ask, "Was it awful?"

She nods and flops into one of the cushy chairs. "A nightmare. We only got back ten minutes ago."

I can hear the shower start up in the bathroom, but I still drop my voice because if I know Mrs. McKenze, she does not want Marissa talking about it. "You couldn't get him out?"

She sits up a little. "The jail is *huge*. They kept sending us around to different places, and we had to go through tons of security and lock up our stuff 'cause you're not allowed to bring in a cell phone or food or water or *anything*. And we couldn't just go in and see him. First we had to register, then we had to schedule a 'visit,' then we paid his bail and waited around for the 'visit'—"

"Why are you saying it like that?"

"I thought a visit would be like in the movies. You know, where the sheriff takes you back and you can talk to people through metal bars? But it wasn't anything like that. We went into this big room with a bunch of open booths where we finally got to do a virtual visit."

"You mean like on a computer?"

"Yes! He could see us and we could see him—Sammy, he looked *terrible*."

"Could you talk to him, or did you have to type, or what?"

"No, you talk over a phone while you look at a computer screen. But everyone can hear what you're saying! And Mom and Dad got in a big fight over the fact that Mom brought me and . . . and"—her face crinkles up—"it was awful!"

I shake my head. "Maybe your mom didn't know what she was getting you into?"

"She didn't. She said if she had known, she would never have brought me."

"So . . . now what? When does he get out?"

"Sometime after ten tomorrow morning." She sits up a little and says, "Sammy, once he's out, we're leaving. And Mom says there's no way she's letting you stay here alone."

"Like in this room? Or in Las Vegas."

"Either." She gives me a pinchy little look. "I take it you didn't get anywhere?"

"Actually, I might have a lead," I tell her, racking my brains about what in the world I'm going to do.

Her eyebrows go flying. "Really?"

"Yeah," I laugh. "Elvis is helping out."

"Wait, Elvis is? You mean the Elvis who used to work at Maynard's? You actually *found* him?"

"Mm-hmm. And guess what? He's got connections all over town and thinks he'll be able to track her down."

"Seriously?"

"Yup!"

To me I sound way too enthused, but Marissa's so wiped out she doesn't notice. "Wow. So . . . how long will that take?"

"He's on it now. I'm supposed to check in in a few hours."

She squints at me. "Like, at three in the morning?"

"Uh-huh. He's doing his Elvis thing down on the Strip. Said he'd be up all night."

I guess I'd woven in enough truth, because she just says, "Wow."

"So I should probably set an alarm, huh?" And as I'm checking out the clock next to the couch, I add, "Man, I'm wiped out. Aren't you?"

"I don't think I've ever been this tired in my life."

Just then Mrs. McKenze comes into the room with a towel wrapped around her hair. She's got puffy eyes, too, but tries to smile when she sees me. "Oh, hi, Sammy. You had us worried."

"I'm sorry. I did leave a note. I just went to get some food." Then I add, "Thanks again for letting me crash on your couch."

She looks from me to Marissa and back again. "You being here is actually a blessing." She comes over and gives Marissa a kiss on the forehead. "I'm so sorry I put you through this. It was a horrible idea."

"You didn't know, Mom."

She stands there a minute, then says, "Well, I'll see you in the morning."

"Good night," we tell her, and after Marissa hangs out for a few more minutes, she finds me a blanket and a pillow and drags herself to bed, too.

Now, the truth is, I *am* wiped out. And I really don't know what to do, but I'm sure not ready to leave Las Vegas yet. I mean, I found Elvis, right? He was out there connecting with . . . connections for me, right? And if Marissa's mom was going to make me go home with them in the morning, it would be a total waste of everything I'd gone through!

So I pretend to go to bed, but my head's whirring around for some way to not get dragged home. It crosses my mind to call Casey—more because I want to let him know what's going on than because I think his mom's told him anything new—but all of a sudden an idea whacks me upside the head.

I sit there for a minute just stunned because I know it's crazy.

Scratch that—it's certifiably insane!

And I know it's risky.

Make that treacherously dangerous!

It's also an enormous gamble.

But really, what have I got to lose?

And the more I think about it, the more *sense* it makes.

Besides, I still have Marissa's room key, and I can always come back. . . .

So when I'm sure Marissa and her mom are asleep, I write a note that says, *Found her! See you back at home! Thanks for everything! Love, Sammy.*

Then I slip out the door and head for the elevators.

TEN

Yeah, it was almost one in the morning, and, no, I didn't care.

I knocked hard on the door.

Now, normally I would never wake someone up like this, but a knock on the door at one in the morning didn't come *close* to payback for the things they'd done to me.

No one answered, though, so I knocked again.

And again.

And finally a sleepy voice on the other end goes, "Who is it?"

"Urgent message," I call through the door. "About the wedding."

The chain slides off and the door flies open, and there I am, face to face with Heather, who's wearing shiny pink shorts, a white tank top, and a pained squint.

Before she can even register that it's me, I step in and head for the sitting room, which is a lot smaller than the one in Marissa's suite. The whole place is. It's basically one room with a half wall dividing the sleeping area from a small sitting area.

"Mom!" Heather cries like she's in the middle of a horrible nightmare.

Candi clicks on a lamp and sits up in bed, so I know I've got to talk fast. "Look, Heather, I don't want my mom marrying your dad any more than you do. I've met with a guy who has contacts all over Las Vegas. He's going to get in touch with me the minute he finds out where they're getting married." I look her right in the eye. "Once I get the call, I'm thinking you and I should crash the wedding and stop them."

Heather's wide-awake now, and her Eternal Fire of Hate has sparked back to life. "We don't need *you* to help *us* stop this stupid wedding!"

Which brings me to the moment of the Enormous Gamble.

"Oh . . . so you already know where and when they're getting married?" I ask as I head back toward the door. "What a relief! Obviously I was worried about nothing." I give her a little smile. "I know you'll do a dandy job of messing the whole thing up all by yourself, so . . . see ya!"

"Wait!" Candi cries, hurrying toward me.

I stop and turn and casually raise an eyebrow.

Candi clicks on another light. Her copper hair's sticking out in spots, and it's the first time I've seen her with no makeup on. She looks really different. Really pale.

"So you're not here *with* your mother?" she asks.

"Actually, I'm here against her. I want to stop the wedding as much as you do." I give Heather a cheesy smile. "Weird to be on the same side, huh?"

Heather cries, "We're not on the same side!" and Candi

jumps in with, "What makes you so sure we're here to stop the wedding?"

I give Candi a look like, Du-uh, and then Heather's back in with, "Why are we even talking to you? You can't come busting into someone's room at one in the morning!" She flashes the evil eye at her mother. "I *told* you not to tell Casey!"

"I didn't tell him!"

Heather points an angry finger at me. "Then how did she know where to find us?"

Candi cries, "*Casey* doesn't know, so how could he tell her?"

I break up their little argument by saying, "I'm not here because of Casey. I'm here because my mother's marrying your dad and I figured you didn't want to be stepsisters any more than I do. I also figured you'd be up all night trying to track them down like I've been, but you're *not,* so obviously you know where they are and when the wedding is." I start for the door again. "And since you've got it under control, I'll call off my guy and leave you to it. Like I said, I know you'll do a great job messing up their little plans."

"Wait!" Candi cries again, cutting me off at the door.

"Mom, no!" Heather shouts, like she's scolding a dog.

Candi shoots Heather a look, then gives me a really pained smile. Like just the effort might kill her. "Let's talk," she says, easing me back toward the sitting area. "So . . . your mother didn't include you in her plans, either?"

I shake my head.

"Hurtful, isn't it?"

I give her a little nod and let her sit me on the couch.

But Heather and I have known each other long enough for her to be onto what I'm doing. "Mom," she says through her teeth, "she's working you."

Her mom gives her a sly look back, and even though I'm pretending to look down, I totally catch it.

No, honey, *I'm* working *her.*

"So," Candi says, sitting beside me, "tell me about your networking contact."

I give a little shrug. "He lives here. He marries people. I met with him tonight, and he's put the word out about my mom."

She eyes me suspiciously. "Why would he agree to do that?"

I shrug again. "He's a friend."

"A friend," she says, like I've just told her he's the president.

"Mm-hmm. And he's into celebrities, so . . ." I just let that drift off into the air, because I know Candi is green over my mom being on TV.

"Where's your dad in all of this?" she asks, her eyes sort of whittling me down.

"Oh, well. That's a whole 'nother story." I start to stand up, saying, "Anyway, let her have it tomorrow." I look at Heather. "I mean it. And give her some from me, too, would you?"

"Wait!" Candi says, and actually grabs my arm and pulls me back onto the couch. "Who are you here with?"

I look her straight in the eye. "Nobody."

"Liar," Heather sneers.

I shrug like, Whatever.

Candi looks at my backpack and skateboard. "So . . . where are you staying?"

"I thought I might stay *here*," I tell her with a little laugh, "but since you don't need my help, I'm sure I'm not welcome."

Heather and her mother have a little tug-of-war of spastic looks, and in the end Heather just comes out and says, "No! You cannot let her stay here!"

"Oh!" I say, jumping up like I'm surprised that's what they were having their little cross fire about. "No, Heather's right. It was a very bad idea."

"Could we get your cell number?" Candi asks. "In case we want to get in touch?"

"I don't have a cell."

"You don't?" She looks at her daughter like she can't believe I'm telling the truth, but Heather just shrugs like, Yeah, it's true.

I tell them, "Well, I've gotta go find a pay phone and call off my friend. Sorry for waking you up."

"Wait!" Candi says, yanking me back *again*. Then she blurts out, "Look, we *don't* know where they're getting married and—"

"Noooooo!" Heather wails, but her mother scolds her with, "Quit it! If we're going to stop this wedding in time, we need to work together."

"Oh," I say, looking like I've just found a nasty bruise on my very shiny apple. "You don't know where they're getting married? So"—I blink at her a bunch—"what *do* you know?"

"Not much," she says with a frown.

"So . . . why am I working with you?"

It's her turn to blink at me. "Because I have a couch?"

"Well," I scoff, like that's no big deal. "Do you have a *car*?"

"Yes! We drove here!"

My jaw is in serious danger of clunking to the floor. I mean, it's no secret that Candi is a maniac behind the wheel, but if they *drove* from Santa Martina? She must've been going, like, a hundred and twenty the whole way.

Still, I do my best to keep it smooth as I ask, "And . . . what about *your* cell phone? Since I don't have one, could my friend call yours when he has something to report?"

"Of course!"

I pull the photo card of my mother out of my backpack. "I've been using this. . . . Do you have a picture of Warren?"

"Of Warren," she says, like I've just crossed the line with that one.

"Well, of your ex."

She doesn't seem to like that any better.

"You know—Heather's dad? My gonna-be dad? The groom-to-be? The—"

"Warren!" she snaps. "Warren is fine."

"Didn't mean to offend," I tell her quietly. "This is just a really weird situation."

"You've got that right."

"So?" I ask. "Do you?"

"Do I what?"

"Have a picture?"

She hesitates, then shakes her head.

But Heather's scrolling through her phone and she says, "I do."

I've seen pictures on Heather's phone before, and let me tell you, they're not the kind you'd want to share with your mother.

But this picture was different.

It was sweet.

Innocent.

It was Heather at about ten, hugging her dad—both her arms thrown around him while he had one wrapped around her. They both looked so happy. And what's funny is, even if I hadn't known either of them, I'd have known that this was a picture of a dad and his daughter. Not a dad and his niece, or a coach and a player, or a couple of actors.

This was a dad who adored his daughter, just like the daughter adored her dad.

In that moment I felt almost sorry for Heather. Somewhere along the line she'd lost the joy that was obviously there in that picture, and now she was just . . . sour. But I also felt sorry for me. Seeing the joy of Heather being with her dad made me realize that I would never, ever have a picture like that of me and my dad.

And then Heather pulls her phone away and says, "What are you staring at, loser?" which brings me back to the realities of dealing with an evil psychopath instead of finding excuses for why she'd become one.

Candi hadn't even looked at the picture. Instead, she'd been fixated on me. "Are we agreed, then?" she asks.

"Sure," I tell her, like I could go either way.

She hands me her cell phone. "Then call your contact and set it up."

So I dig up Pete's number, punch it into Candi's phone, and when he answers, I say, "It's Sammy. The number I'm calling you from is the number to reach me at. But it's not my phone, and we need to come up with a password, okay?"

"A password?"

"Yeah." I eye Heather. "I've made a dangerous alliance, and it's possible someone might pretend to be me."

Heather flips me off, which doesn't seem to faze Candi at all.

"So what's the password?" Pete says in my ear.

"If you call me or if I call you, the first thing you need to do is list some Elvis songs. I'll say no to anything but the right one. And only you and I know the right one."

"So what's the right one?"

"You tell me."

"How about 'Love Me Tender'?"

"Perfect."

"So I go in random order?"

"Right. Mix it up every time we talk."

"Got it. Oh, and hey—I've got help out there. The Elvis Army's rallyin'."

"You're serious? Cool!"

"Later, gator."

"No, really?"

He laughs and hangs up.

"Very clever," Candi says as I hand the phone back to her.

I give her a little smile. "I do want to survive the night."

So they go back to bed, and I curl up on the couch, and the truth is, I'm hugely relieved. I have a place to stay, I have two people helping me—one with the most determined mind I've ever gone up against—and there's an Elvis Army out on the streets of Las Vegas rallying.

Whatever that means.

I put my head down on my backpack pillow, too exhausted to care.

ELEVEN

I had a really frightening dream that night.

Heather Acosta was being *nice* to me.

It was one of those total anxiety dreams. You know—like when you're searching for something and can't find it?

I was searching for her angle.

What was she up to?

Why was she being so nice to me?

I knew it was a trap. I mean, it *had* to be a trap. But where was the trapdoor? Why couldn't I see it? Any second I was going to step into it and—*aaaaahhhh!*—I'd fall into a deep, dark abyss, and she'd be laughing at me from above, going, "Looooooooooser!" as I tumbled down, down, down to my death.

So I kept trying to figure it out, and she kept being nice to me.

And then, like a nightmare within a nightmare, I hear, "Looooooooooser! Hey, looooooooooser."

I couldn't see her; all I could hear was her voice.

"Hey, loser!"

I flailed around, looking, looking, looking.

And then she was shoving me.

Hard.

I flailed around some more.

Why couldn't I see her?

And then I realized—oh yeah, my eyes are closed.

They popped open, but everything was still dark.

Only not *as* dark.

And then all of a sudden it was super bright and there was Heather, holding back the curtain, blinding me with white-hot Las Vegas sunshine.

She was still wearing her silky pink pajama shorts and her sneer, and she was holding out a cell phone.

I guess I was having a little trouble transitioning from dream to reality because she finally says, "Take it!"

So I take the phone and put it up to my ear. "Hello?"

" 'Suspicious Minds'?"

"Huh?"

There was silence for a second and then, "Sammy?"

"Yeah."

" 'Suspicious Minds' is an Elvis song."

"Oh!" I finally sit up and snap to. "Right! I mean, no, wrong!"

"Did I wake you up?"

"Yeah, sorry."

"I can tell that's you—can we cut to the chase?"

"No. Make sure. Always make sure."

"All right, all right," he says like Elvis. " 'Love Me Tender.' "

"Yes."

"Thank you, Miss Sammy."

"So what have you got?"

"They do not have an appointment at any of the bigger chapels and—more important—they haven't applied for a license in the state of Nevada."

"They—how do you know *that*?"

"I told you I was on it," he says with a laugh. But then he adds, "That doesn't mean they can't be walkin' up to the counter right now, though."

"Is it open already?" I look around for a clock but don't see one anywhere. "What time is it?"

"Bedtime for me, ten-thirty for you."

"Ten-thirty?"

"Guess you had the dark shades drawn?"

"Yeah."

He laughs. "Welcome to Las Vegas, little mama."

It sounds like he's about to hang up, so I blurt out, "Wait! Where's this counter?"

"The marriage counter? At the Marriage Bureau. It's downtown."

"You think I should stake it out?"

He hesitates. "I knew you were smart. Yes. If they're coming to Vegas to get hitched, they have to get a license first. That'd be *the* place to stake out."

"Thank you!" I tell him. And then, because he always said it to me when I bought stuff from him at Maynard's Market, I do my best Elvis impersonation and add, "Thank you very much."

He laughs and hangs up, and since I'm feeling pretty psyched, I'm laughing, too, when I click off.

And then I see Heather.

She's standing there with her angry arms crossed and

her signature sneer. "So? What did he tell you? Huh, loser?"

I study her a minute. "Can you mix it up a little with the insults? You know, throw in an 'idiot' or a 'dimwit' or a 'lame-brained bozo'? The 'loser' thing is really getting old."

She snatches the phone from me. "You can't tell me what to call you, loser!"

I scratch my head. "Just a suggestion, sis."

"Shut up!" she screeches.

Candi comes over and snatches the phone from Heather and says, "You're making this way harder than it needs to be." Now, at first I think she's talking to both of us, but she keeps her eyes on Heather. "Just drop the name-calling altogether. We have work to do!" Then she turns to me and says, "Please tell us what you found out."

A "please"?

Wow.

I sit up taller on the couch and tell her, "They're not registered at any of the bigger chapels—"

"But what if they're going to a small one? And they could walk up at any time!"

"Right. *But* they haven't applied for a marriage license yet. Not in the state of Nevada, anyway."

"But . . . they can do that at any time, too! There's no waiting period or blood tests or any of that in Nevada. That's why people come here!"

"Right, but they haven't done it *yet*, which means that if we stake out the Marriage Bureau, we can confront them before they even get their license!"

Now, I'm actually really excited about this break-through, and for a second there I've lost track of the fact that I'm talking to my archenemy's nasty-tempered mother. So I'm, like, bouncing a little and, you know, wide-eyed and happy.

Like I'd be if I were talking to a friend.

But then it registers that her face is all pinchy and her eyes are like little laser beams, staring at me, so I stop bouncing and start thinking about diving for cover. And then out of her pinchy, laser-beamy face comes a loud, hard hiss.

A hiss that it takes me a minute to realize is her saying, "Yes!"

Now, even though I *think* this means that she's excited, too, it's creepy enough that I'm not actually sure. So I say, "Good, huh?"

"Exxxcellent!" she says, hissing again.

Which, let me tell you, is more than a little scary.

"You're doing it again, Mom," Heather says under her breath.

Candi snaps out of it. "I am?"

"Yeah," Heather tells her. "It's really creepy."

Candi turns to me. "Was I . . . hissing?"

I look at her, then sort of glance at Heather, thinking it might be really wise of me to just not say. But Heather gives a little smirk with a one-shoulder shrug, which is pretty much universal for, Go ahead—tell her.

So I tell her. "Yeah. You were hissing."

She blinks like she has no memory at all of going snaky on me. "And it was creepy?"

I glance at Heather again, and again I get the little smirk-shrug thing.

"Yeah," I tell Candi. "Kinda."

"Not kinda," Heather snaps. "Tell her!"

So I pull a little face and tell Candi, "Let's just say you're a lot prettier when you don't hiss."

Now, the truth is, Candi puts a lot of effort into trying to make herself look pretty. She's a flashy dresser and isn't afraid of makeup, but underneath all that makeup is a slightly droopy eye, and a sort of knotty chin. Not knotty like a big ol' sailor rope or anything. More just knotty like a walnut.

Not a *huge* walnut.

More just a, you know, *junior* walnut.

Not that I'd ever *noticed* her knotty chin before—I'd actually never been this close to her before. The other times I'd seen her, I'd either ducked or run . . . or been sitting across the conference table from her in the school office having bigger things to worry about than droopy eyes and knotty chins.

Anyway, Candi's head bobbles a little, and that's the end of the hissing debate. She hurries back to the bedroom area saying, "Get ready, girls. We've got a destination!"

Well, since I'd only crammed the bare necessities into my backpack before I'd bolted out of the apartment, after a little water splashing, teeth scrubbing, and raking through the hair, I'm ready to go. And Heather actually doesn't take too long, either. But Candi? She's in that bathroom for what feels like an *hour*.

It feels that way partly because Heather and I are holed

up in our separate corners, avoiding each other, and partly because I'm really hungry and I can hear Heather in the bedroom munching on stuff. I know she's not going to offer me any, but I don't feel like I can go to the food court to get myself something to eat, because knowing Candi and Heather, they'd ditch me now that they had a plan.

Plus, I didn't know what time Marissa and her mom would be leaving, and I sure didn't want to run into them.

So finally I break down and ask, "Could I maybe have a little of that?"

"Could you maybe not talk to me?"

So I just sit there with my stomach grumbling, listening to Heather munch and crunch. Then things go quiet, and pretty soon I catch a whiff of cigarette smoke. So I spy around the divider, and sure enough, she's smoking, keeping the end of the cigarette out a small slit in the window as she puffs from it, then blows smoke outside through the opening.

When she's done, she flicks the butt out, then closes the window and sprays cologne around all over the place.

When Candi finally emerges from the bathroom, her face is all done up and she has high heels on. "Are you girls ready?"

"For like an *hour*," Heather grumbles.

So we head out to the elevators and down to the first floor. I am starving, so real quick I duck into the little store by the water fountain and buy a box of Double Stuff Oreos and a carton of milk. Then I race to catch up to Heather and her mother because they'd just kept on walking.

I spot them about halfway across the lobby, and since

there was no way I was going to leave my stuff locked inside Heather's hotel room when I don't have a key, it's really tempting to put down my skateboard and *ride* across the huge lobby, but catching up to them on foot is a piece of cake, so I don't.

After we've crossed the lobby, Candi leads us down the escalator and through the little tunnel mall. But it isn't until we're outside and Candi pulls over to light up a cigarette that Heather notices I'm eating Oreos and swigging milk. "Why'd you want my food when you had your own?"

"Uh . . . I just now got these?"

"Yeah, right. Where?"

I feel like saying, I'd tell you but you told me not to talk to you, remember? But I figure why make things worse? So I say, "At that little store by the waterfall."

"While we were walking?" She sneers at me. "Liar."

"Heather!" Candi snaps. "Quit with the names."

"Well, what would *you* call her? There's no way she went into a store and bought cookies and milk without us knowing!"

Candi drags on her cigarette and eyes me like, Well?

So I tell her, "I was starving. I hustled." And because she's still eyeing me, I add, "You're in heels. I'm in high-tops. It wasn't hard." Then I hold out the box of cookies to Heather. "Want one?"

"No!" Heather snaps. "Don't even act like my friend, 'cause you're not!"

I laugh. "It's a cookie, Heather."

But she's right. It's more than a cookie. I mean, how can you feud when you're twisting apart Oreos?

It'd be like breaking bread with the enemy.

So I take back the offer, and when Candi grinds the stub of her cigarette into the cement and tells me, "No food in my car," I start double-stuffing *myself*, 'cause who knows when I'll get the next chance to eat. Plus, all of a sudden I'm nervous. I mean, getting into Candi Acosta's little red sports car is like hitching a ride on a flaming bullet.

What was I getting myself into?

It raced through my mind that I really ought to find some other way to get to the Marriage Bureau, but I didn't know my way around at all, and from my little two-block walk last night, I had the hunch it would take me all day to get downtown.

I didn't even know which direction downtown was.

So when we get to Candi's car and Heather tilts the front seat forward, I crawl in back.

Then Candi fires up the motor and peels out, laying rubber and centrifuging us around turns as she tears out of the parking structure and onto the street.

TWELVE

I just kept quiet in the backseat while Heather tapped the screen of her mother's phone and gave her mom directions. "No, stay on Tropicana! We have to get on Fifteen North."

Not having a cell phone at all, I was having a really hard time not looking over the headrest at what she was doing with hers. And the truth is, I was jealous.

Really jealous.

And it didn't take long for me being jealous over a cell phone to turn into reinforced anger at my mother. Pete was right—her life compared to mine was just *wrong*.

"Get back, loser. I don't like you breathing down my neck."

I guess at that moment I was mad enough at my mother that it didn't register that I'd just been called a loser or, really, who I was sitting behind. Because out of my mouth comes a pathetic little "Sorry."

"Heather!" Candi snaps. "The names are unnecessary."

Heather snorts. "You're right. I was stating the obvious."

"Heather!"

For some reason this seems to put Heather in a righteously bad mood. She snarls and snaps directions at her mother, and when we get back off the freeway and Candi misses a turn, Heather cries, "That was Clark! Right there!" Then she grumbles, "Great. Now we have to go clear around the block." And that's when what's *really* bothering her comes out. "I don't know why we had to take her with us. Why is she even here? We know what to do. We don't need her!"

Candi downshifts and roars through a yellow light. "Strength in numbers."

"What?"

"Heather, you throwing another one of your tantrums is not going to convince your father of anything. Both of you being here might."

"*Tantrums?* I can't believe you just said that!" Heather shrieks. "And in front of *her*."

"She's not the one giving me a headache right now," Candi mutters as she guns it down the street.

"*What?*"

Now, normally I would have been hanging on every word of this spat, but right then I notice CLARK COUNTY DETENTION CENTER on the huge gray building that we've been circling, and out of my little window I see Marissa and her mom and dad getting into their rental car.

At first I can't believe it's them, and then I feel like I'm watching them in slo-mo, even though we're zooming by. Marissa's dad looks awful. His clothes are a mess, and he seems pretty green around the gills. Like any minute he's going to bend over and barf. And while Mrs. McKenze's acting really uptight—a no-nonsense get-in-the-car-I-want-*out*-of-here kind of uptight—Marissa seems dazed, very pale and sort of stunned.

I want to call out to her. I want to bail out *for* her. But I'm a prisoner in the back of this blazing bullet and before you know it we're half a block past them and Candi's crying, "There it is!" and cutting across traffic and into a big, open, mostly empty parking lot.

So wait, I say to myself, the Marriage Bureau and the jail are on the same block? And at that moment I make a weird connection in my head.

A connection between Marissa and me and Heather.

And I guess it kind of knocks me upside the head, because out of my mouth pops, "Man, parents can really mess you up."

"Shut up!" Heather practically spits, twisting around to face me. "Stay out of it!"

"Heather, what is wrong with you?" Candi says as she nose-dives to a halt in the wide open. "She was *agreeing* with you!"

"I don't need her agreeing with me! And we shouldn't even be talking about him in front of her! I hate her, you get that? And you hate her, too, remember?"

So I guess they'd been talking about Warren, but right then all I could think about was Marissa maybe spotting *us*. Like she didn't have enough on her plate already? I sure didn't want her worrying about me being so desperate that I'd teamed up with Candi and Heather!

I mean, talk about hell freezing over.

And since I didn't know which direction the McKenzes

would be driving or how long it would take them to leave the area, I kind of dragged and fumbled and, you know, *delayed* getting out of the backseat.

"Just *leave* it," Heather says as I'm pretending my skateboard's stuck, and when I pull it out anyway, she mutters, "You are such a dork."

"Look," I tell her. "You want to get rid of me as soon as possible after we find them, right?"

"You got that right!"

"So see? I'm just being optimistic."

"Girls, come on!" Candi says, clicking along in her high heels.

"Stop calling us girls!" Heather snaps.

Candi tosses a look over her shoulder. "You'd rather I called you boys?"

I laugh out loud because coming from Candi it seemed really funny. And for the first time ever Candi grins at me.

Heather catches up to her mother and cries, "That was not funny! None of this is funny!"

I felt like I'd moved from being a prisoner to being someone tossed in the middle of a battleground. Why couldn't we just get the job done and *be* done? Why all this sniping and tension and fighting?

With Heather there were always battles, but after all this time I still had no idea what had actually started our war. Heather had just hated me from day one.

Something about my shoes.

And for the past year and a half we'd moved from battle to battle to battle, but . . . why?

We're at the Marriage Bureau now, and Candi is just

reaching for the door when her phone goes off. We stop and look at Heather, who's still holding it, and Heather gives herself away by glancing at me before she steps aside to answer it. "Hello?"

Candi abandons the door and follows Heather, so I follow, too, and when Heather says, "Yup, it's me," I call out, "No, it's not!"

Heather hunches over like she's trying to protect the phone from my voice and says, "No . . . no . . . yes." Then she lets out a little curse and hands me the phone.

"Hey, it's me," I say into it.

"I'm too tired to play this game, but in case you're another imposter, here we go again: 'In the Ghetto.'"

"No."

"'Don't Cry Daddy.'"

"No."

"'Peace in the Valley.'"

"I wish . . . but no."

"'Amazing Grace.'"

"Definitely not."

"'Love Me Tender.'"

"Bingo."

He lets out a heavy sigh. "I just got a call. There's been a sighting."

"There *has?*"

"Uh-huh. Inside the Miracle Mile Shops. They're at Oyster Annie's having lunch."

"Oyster Annie's?" I was picturing a girl in a big rubber hat and boots. It sounded like the last place on earth my mother would go.

"Yeah. Now go catch her, would you? The King needs his beauty rest."

"Thank you!"

I click off, and once again I'm so excited that I forget who I'm working with. "There's been a sighting!"

"There *has?*" Candi asks all bug-eyed, and even Heather perks up.

"Do you know where the Miracle Mile Shops are?"

"Yes!" Candi says. "It's a giant mall on the Strip."

"Well, let's go!" I tell them. "They're at Oyster Annie's."

"Oyster Annie's?" they say with disgust.

I laugh. "It's a restaurant."

Candi squints at me. "Warren doesn't eat *oysters.*"

And I'm so excited that we've got a real lead that I joke back with "Probably my mother's bad influence?" which makes Candi roll her eyes, but a little grin does actually break through.

But heading back to the car, I start thinking that I really *can't* picture my mom eating oysters. Or going any-where . . . oystery. And then I start worrying that maybe it's a false sighting. Maybe we should stay and stake out the Marriage Bureau. Or maybe we should split up, with one of us waiting here and the others going to the mall.

But . . . who would go where?

Not an easy thing to figure out when you factor in the possibility of being backstabbed—something Heather's a master at.

But before I know it, we're back in the car, and we're zooming down a street, blasting past giant billboards about bail bonds and half-price lawyers.

"Look at all these stupid wedding chapels," Heather grumbles after we've gone a few blocks. And she's right—every other building is a wedding chapel. And since I'm kinda leaning forward again so I can see better, it's easy for her to turn and tell me, "Getting married here is cheap. And tacky."

"And legally binding," Candi says, stepping on the gas.

I just sit there for a minute, and finally I say, "What I don't get—"

"Don't talk to us, you get *that*?" Heather snaps, turning all the way around in her seat.

"Fine!" I tell her, sitting back. "I was just feeling sorry for your mom, okay?"

Candi eyes me in the mirror. "Why's that?"

" 'Cause you're obviously still in love with him."

"You are *so* out of line," Heather says. "And stupid!" She looks at her mom. "Can you *believe* her?" She vultures around at me. "Now stop talking to us!"

"Fine." Then I mutter, "But your mom's still in love with your dad."

"Stop it!"

"Fine."

But even when I'm quiet, Heather can't seem to let it go. She stays vultured and finally points at me and says, "Stop it!"

"What? What am I doing?"

"Stop thinking that!"

"What am I thinking?!"

"You know what you're thinking and so do I, so stop it! You don't know anything about anything!"

113

Now, this whole time Candi hasn't said a word, but she has glanced back at me in the mirror.

Like six times.

Which is a lot, considering how she's darting through traffic.

But what's really weird about the whole situation is that what I said seems to be news to Candi, too. Like she really thought she was here to stop her ex from marrying the mother of her daughter's archenemy for her *daughter's* sake.

And then we're squealing through a parking structure, going up, up, up, until Candi finds a slot she likes and nose-dives into it. "Let's go, girls," she says, flying out of the car and over to the elevators.

The Miracle Mile Mall is huge—like an enclosed little city of shops. But Candi's jaw's not dropped like mine. She beelines for a directory, and when she finds Oyster Annie's, she says, "Come on!" And as she hurries ahead, I hear her hiss, "There's no stopping us now!"

THIRTEEN

The main corridor of the mall is like a shiny wide esplanade, with big fountains and park benches and enormous potted plants decorating it. It has shops on both sides and gradually curves to the right. And as Heather and I try to keep up with Candi, I start feeling like this shiny wide esplanade is a track and I'm in some crazy race where I'm somehow stuck in last place. Sure, I've got my backpack and a skateboard weighing me down, but not being able to keep up with a woman in heels?

So I'm kind of relieved when Candi comes skidding to a halt, looks around quick, then heads back toward a little cul-de-sac of shops off to the side. "There it is!" she cries, and charges toward Oyster Annie's, where a girl in a skimpy sailor dress is standing behind a hostess podium. But when we're about thirty feet from the restaurant, Candi sort of sputters to a stop and just stands there, staring.

"Mom? Do you see them?" Heather asks, and we both scan the little groups of tables set up outside the main part of the restaurant, trying to spot our wayward parents.

The tables are roped off by fishing nets with fake crabs and seagulls and red-and-white buoys. It's supposed to look like outdoor dining, because there's a splish-splashy, tugboat-tooty sound track playing, only we're standing inside a mall on a shiny floor under fluorescent lights, so something about the whole setup is . . . weird.

"Mom?" Heather says. "Where are they?"

Candi's head sort of shivers. "What?" She looks at Heather. "Oh."

"Mo-om! What is wrong with you?"

"You girls go in. I'll wait here."

Heather squints at her. *"What?"*

"Go on," Candi says. "It would look bad if I . . . if I . . . went in."

"But—"

"Come on," I tell Heather, and hurry for the entrance because Sailor Girl has just gone inside to seat another party and it's the perfect time to sail in right behind them.

"Wait!" Heather says, yanking on my sleeve.

"Be cool," I tell her back, and once we're inside, I split away from the group that's being seated. "Just act like you know where you're going."

"Don't tell me to be cool," she says through her teeth, "and don't tell me how to act!"

"Fine. You go that way," I say, pointing into a separate area of the restaurant, "and I'll go this way."

"And don't tell me where to go! There's no way I'm letting you find them first!"

"Oh, good grief," I mutter.

"That is the stupidest expression. And you use it all

116

the time! That and 'holy smokes.' They don't *mean* anything!"

I stop short and turn to face her. "Could you give it a rest for just one minute and help me look?" I start moving again. "And do you know what you're going to say when we find them? We should have a plan, don't you think?"

"A plan," she says, like it's the stupidest thing anyone's ever said. "You think us being here doesn't say it all?"

And then I get a bright idea. "Hey! What if we act like we're here on our own?"

"You mean . . . like my mom isn't with us?"

"Yeah! They'd have to take, you know, parental responsibility, right? You can't just let your kids wander around Las Vegas alone. It's like . . . reckless abandonment or child endangerment or . . ." I laugh. "Or something!"

Heather's face doesn't light up like, *Brilliant,* or anything. But her sneer doesn't show up, either. She just *stares* at me a minute, then snaps to and says, "Whatever. Let's just find them."

So we cruise through the restaurant, which sort of horseshoes past a long bar and into another section and back to the front of the restaurant.

"They're not here," Heather snarls. "Your tip was bogus!" Then she grabs me and spins me around. "Who is that guy, anyway?"

"What guy?"

"That guy who calls you! Are you just making him up?"

"How could I be making him up? You talked to him!"

"Yeah, but he's probably just one of your dorky friends!

There's no way *you* have some informant in Las Vegas. And how convenient that he 'spotted' them. You don't just happen to spot someone in Las Vegas! You're probably making this whole thing up!"

"Why would I do that?"

"So you could torture me!"

I roll my eyes and head for Sailor Girl, who's back at the podium. "Believe it or not, I've got better things to do than come up with ways to torture you."

"Yeah, like what?" she says, grabbing me again.

"You're serious?"

"Yeah! I think you're making this whole thing up!"

I yank free and shake my head. "Oh, good grief."

"See! There you go again with that stupid saying!"

We're at the podium now, so I swing off my backpack, pull out my mother's picture card, and hand it to Sailor Girl. "I'm trying to catch up with my mother. . . . Was she just here?"

Sailor Girl takes the card and breaks into a smile. "Yes!" She hands it back and says, "Your dad—"

"He's not her dad, he's *my* dad!" Heather snaps.

Sailor Girl's mouth goes into a little O, and after a short hesitation where she seems to be sizing up the situation, she says, "Well, lucky you. He's handsome *and* charming. A real gentleman."

"Do you know which way they went?" I ask, trying to get back on track. She shakes her head and gives a little shrug, so I hitch my backpack back on my shoulder and say, "How long ago did they leave?"

"Maybe ten minutes?"

"Thanks!" I tell her, then jet over to Candi, who's looking like she's trapped in some invisible cage.

"Well?" Candi asks.

"We just missed them," I tell her.

"So now what?" Heather says, sneering at me like it's all my fault.

So I say, "Well, we came in that way and didn't see them, right?" but Heather shuts me down by snapping, "I'm not asking *you*, loser!"

"Heather, *stop*," Candi tells her. "Sammy's right. We would have seen them, so they must have gone that way!"

Heather wobbles her head at her mother. "Oh yeah? What if they went inside a store? We would have walked right by them!"

Now, the way she said it was so snotty that I didn't want it to be true, but she was right—we could easily have just not seen them. "So what do you want to do?"

"Split up," Heather says. "You go that way, we'll go this way."

"Okaaaay," I tell her. "But you'll have to lend me your phone."

"There's no way I'm lending you my phone!"

"So . . . what if I spot them? How will I tell you?"

"Find a pay phone!"

"When's the last time you saw a pay phone? No, if I find them, I'll talk to them myself—is that what you want?"

"No!"

"Right. We're supposed to be working together. So can you quit hating me long enough to get this done?"

She gives me one of her hard stares until Candi says, "I agree we should split up, but unlike *some* parents, I'm not letting my daughter wander around Las Vegas by herself." She turns to Heather. "You and Sammy go that way, I'll go around the other way. We'll text or call each other to stay in touch. Just stick together!"

Heather tries arguing, but finally her mother snaps, "It's the only thing that makes sense, so just do it! We're wasting time!"

So we head out, hurrying along the shiny esplanade, looking in windows. But I'm feeling like we're both way behind where they might be and that we're doing a lousy job of checking out stores. Plus there are shops on both sides of the walk, and jetting back and forth is not very efficient. So I finally tell Heather, "If you take that side, and I do this side, it'll go a lot faster."

But she won't. And I don't get why. I also don't get why she stays like half a pace behind me the whole time instead of leading. It's like she's my shadow, and talk about being afraid of your own shadow—you do not want Heather Acosta sneaking around behind you! Plus, her being back there is reminding me of the times she's tried following me home from school or the mall. It really bugs her that she doesn't know where I live, but luckily the times she's tailed me I've been. able to ditch her.

Her knowing I live with Grams would be a disaster.

Anyway, not only is her being a few steps behind me really inefficient, it's also making me a little nervous. So after zigzagging between stores a few more times, I finally say, "I'm not going to ditch you, if that's what you're worried about."

"About you ditching me?"

"Yeah. Like when you try to follow me home?"

Her cheeks flush. "Why would I follow a loser like you?"

I give her a casual shrug. "Because I'm *not* a loser, and you'd probably like to torch my house."

"See how stupid you are?"

I stop and face her. "So you tell *me*, then."

She crosses her arms. "I've never followed you home."

"I know," I laugh, "because I've ditched you!"

"I've never followed you at all!"

"Oh, please." I shake my head and say, "Look, why can't you just tell the truth? Why can't you just say something like, I don't think it's fair that you know where I live and I don't know where you live! I don't think it's fair that you can knock on my window on Saturday morning and wake me up, but I can't do that to you!?"

"Yeah!" she cries. "Exactly!"

I smile. "See? I get that. I wouldn't like it, either."

First she just stands there blinking at me, then she sputters, "So?"

"So, what?"

"So, where do you live?"

I laugh again and start walking. "How about I just forget where you live and we'll call it even."

"You can't magically forget where I live! It's in that stupid little brain of yours, and it's not coming out!"

I raise an eyebrow at her. "It's not a stupid little brain,

Heather." Then I add, "But see? I do get it. What I *don't* get is why you can't just *say* that. Why do you have to lie and deny and be so mad all the time?"

She's walking beside me now and says, "Because it's not fair."

I look at her and ask, "What's not fair?" because it seems like she's talking about more than just me knowing where she lives.

"Any of it."

I kind of do a double take at her because her voice sounds so . . . small. And in all the time I've known Heather Acosta, if there's one thing her voice has never even come *close* to sounding, it's small.

But before I can figure out what to say, she snaps, "Quit staring at me and start looking for your mother! And why aren't you showing people that picture of her? We'll never find them at this rate!"

"Right," I say with a nod. "How about I show my mom's picture around on this side of the mall and you show your dad's picture on that side?"

"Fine!" she snaps.

"I promise I won't ditch you!" I call after her, and typical Heather, she flips me off.

After that we hurry along, looking inside stores and showing our pictures to anyone who looks like a good target—salespeople hanging outside their shops or standing near the door, random tourists sitting on benches, the guy selling pretzels in the middle of the walkway—anyone who looks like they've been in one place for a while. Trouble is, we are totally striking out.

And then I step inside a jewelry store.

"May I help you?" a woman in a sky-blue blouse and heaps of jewelry asks.

Now, this is more a jewelry/*art* store, and I can tell she's worried about some ragamuffin girl with a skateboard knocking something over. So I hold out the photo card and say, "Just looking for my mother."

"Your . . ." And then she sees the card. "She was just in here!"

"She was?"

"Yes! She was with a man, admiring the Umber."

"The Umber?"

"The glass cascade statue in the window?"

I turn, and there in the window is what looks like a big, scraggly wig made out of strands of glass.

"She didn't stay long," the lady tells me. "Just a quick question about price. I sensed they had somewhere else to be."

"How long ago were they here?"

"Ten minutes? Maybe less?"

"Do you happen to remember what she was wearing?"

"Hmm. Nothing that really stood out. A gray tunic? But he had on a maroon leather jacket with fringe and beautiful tooling. Never seen one like it."

"Thank you!" And I'm about to leave but at the last minute I stop and ask, "Did you notice any jewelry?"

She laughs. "I do pay attention to jewelry. She wasn't wearing much. A long silver locket, a few bracelets—nothing of any value. He, on the other hand, had a heavy platinum chain on his wrist and Louis Vuitton sunglasses."

"What about rings?"

"Didn't notice any rings."

"Thank you!" I tell her again, then jet out of there. "Heather!" I shout, 'cause I can see her about five stores down looking around all over the place for me. "Heather!" I call louder, and I'm so stupidly excited that I run toward her like she's a long-lost friend instead of my archenemy. "They were in that jewelry store ten minutes ago!"

"Did they buy rings?"

"No! They were looking at art."

"At *art*?"

"Some big glob of glass," I say with a laugh. "But the saleslady told me that they're *not* wearing rings, and that my mom is wearing a gray tunic and your dad is wearing a maroon leather jacket with fringe."

"A maroon leather jacket? With *fringe*?"

"Yeah! And sunglasses."

"Sunglasses?" she says, and although she's squinting at me, it isn't attached to the usual sneer. It's more just a squint of disbelief.

"Yeah, sorry," I tell her, and decide to keep the platinum chain thing to myself. I mean, the times I've seen Warren, he's been a pretty simple dresser, so even the jacket and shades seem like a big change. But my mother did the same thing when she moved to Hollywood, so I add, "My mom's probably been his style coach." Then I spread my arms a little and laugh. "Obviously she hasn't gotten very far with me!" Heather just blinks at me, so I start moving again. "But knowing what they're wearing should help us spot them, right?"

"Right."

We walk along together for a minute before I say, "We should tell your mom, don't you think?"

Her eyes flash at me. "Stop with the 'we' bit. And stop telling me what to do!" She dials her mom, grumbling, "It's so annoying."

I sort of keep my distance while she's talking to her mom, but I do stay close enough to hear what she's saying, which pretty much is just what we've found out. She doesn't sound excited or even annoyed—and unless she's buttering someone up, Heather *always* sounds annoyed. And then after she gets off the phone, she looks down at it for the longest time, and when I edge in closer, I see that she's staring at that picture of her and her dad.

"What's the plan?" I finally ask.

"Keep looking," she says back. Then she asks, "Could I have this side?"

It's just a quiet question. No anger. No hatred. No demand.

I shrug and say, "Sure," and cross over to the other side. And as happy as I am about having gotten more information, in the back of my mind there's also this new, quiet, *sad* feeling.

Not for me.

For Heather.

From the way she's been acting, I'm starting to see a new side to this whole situation. She doesn't want to stop my mom from marrying her dad just because she doesn't want me in her family.

She's also trying to hold on to something that has nothing to do with me.

Something that's already long gone.

FOURTEEN

Heather and I moved from store to store on opposite sides of the shiny walkway, peering through windows, talking to people, and also keeping an eye on each other. I actually got distracted, watching her show her phone picture around. It was like she was desperate for someone, anyone, to say, yes, they'd seen her dad, but all she got were head shakes.

All *I* got were head shakes, too, but I could tell that in Heather's mind it was Sammy 1, Heather 0, and that it was important for her to even the score.

She's *always* trying to even the score.

Even though this time we were supposedly on the same team.

Anyway, I go by a shop with sunglasses displayed on little Plexiglas stands, all spread out and dramatic-looking instead of stacked up on one of those carousels like you see at a regular store. There are huge posters of uber-cool people wearing shades plastered all over the walls and what look like jewelry cases of sunglasses in a horseshoe shape in the middle of the store. And I'm thinking that the store must be doing really bad business because (a) there's nobody in it, and (b) they've got no inventory. I mean, the place could hold *thousands* of sunglasses and what's it got? Maybe a hundred?

A hundred pathetic, lonely sunglasses.

So I'm cruising along with all this flashing through my mind when I see something that makes me do a double take.

Right on the other side of the window, next to a small display of sunglasses, is a silver-and-black sign with two words: LOUIS VUITTON.

A little bell goes ringing in my head, and then I notice that one of the price tags attached to one of the sunglasses in the Louis Vuitton display is faceup instead of facedown, and when I get a closer look, I can't help it—I choke out, "Twelve hundred bucks?" and all of a sudden I'm mad. I mean, what kind of person wastes twelve hundred dollars on a pair of *sunglasses*?

Grams had told me that my mom hadn't saved up anything from being on *Lords*—that she'd been spending it on things that would give her an "aura of success." And now Warren was doing that, too? I could just see Lady Lana cooing in his ear, telling him how great he looked in Louis Vuittons and that he needed to "invest" in his "aura of success."

And I'm so ticked off about my mother and her evil influence on Casey's dad that I turn to find the one person who will totally understand.

Heather.

But when I spot her across the way, I see that she's

talking on her phone. So I zip over in time to hear her say, "See you there."

I hold back what I want to tell her and ask, "Was that your mom?"

"Yeah."

"And?"

"She's at the entrance to Planet Hollywood."

"Who is?" I ask, all excited-like.

"My mother." She rolls her eyes. "God, you're lame."

"I thought you might have meant *my* mother."

"Because your mother is more important than my mother?"

"No! Why do you say stuff like that? I'm actually even more ticked off at my mother right now because . . ." But I stop myself because what in the world am I doing, talking to *Heather*. I mean, I may be ticked off at my mother, but to turn to Heather?

"Because what?" she says when I clam up.

"Never mind."

"Tell me!"

I shake my head.

"That is totally not fair!"

I give her a hard look. "What's not fair is how you always sneer and call me lame or loser and bite my head off and then expect me to tell you something!"

She gives me a hard look back.

So there we are, having a stupid staredown instead of looking for our parents, when something weird and totally unexpected happens.

Heather looks away.

It's not just that she looks away—although that *is* a shock all by itself. It's the *way* she looks away.

Like, Yeah, you're right.

She doesn't *say* that, and it's probably a good thing, because I might have fainted and banged my head on the shiny esplanade floor and *died* if she had. But her losing her hard edge made me soften up, too, and before I know what my mouth is doing, it's going, "Do you know what Louis Vuitton sunglasses are?"

"Yeah . . . why?"

"According to the saleslady in the jewelry store, your dad's wearing a pair."

"Of Louis Vuittons?"

I point across the way. "And according to that store, they sell for twelve hundred bucks."

"Twelve hundred bucks? For *sunglasses*?" Her head wobbles back and forth. "He can't afford that! And if he can, he's sure been doing a good job of hiding it from Mom!"

"My mom's done the same thing. She never sends anything home, because she spends it all on herself."

"Seriously?" She hesitates, then says, "But it's different because your dad's the breadwinner, right? And he's not paying *her* support, is he?"

"Right," I tell her, and change the subject quick. "So where's Planet Hollywood?"

We look around until we find one of those YOU ARE HERE signs and discover that Planet Hollywood Resort and Casino is only a little ways down from where we are, which is good news—but there's also some bad news.

"Look," I say, pointing to different places on the map, "there are five ways out of here!"

Heather studies it a minute. "Which means my dad and your mom could be anywhere."

"Maaaaaan. And we were so close!" It was so frustrating. I'd gone from thinking that Marissa was right—that there was no way I was going to find my mother in this big, crazy city—to being *this* close to catching her.

It was like bobbling a game-winning pop fly.

Candi gives a little wave when she sees us, but there's no smile to go with it. "Dad's wearing Louis Vuitton sunglasses!" Heather blurts out when we get close. "They cost over a thousand dollars!"

Candi's eyebrows stretch waaaaaay up. "How do you know?"

"Sammy found out from the saleslady at the jewelry store! And they're selling Louis Vuitton sunglasses right back there, so we know how much they cost!"

Now, all this was true, and if it had been anyone else, it would have seemed like a perfectly normal way to word things.

But this was Heather.

She *never* called me Sammy.

And the "we" bit?

A small thing.

Just a slip, maybe.

But still.

Huge.

Candi doesn't notice anything different about Heather's words—she's too tuned in to their meaning. Her eyebrows sort of crumble back down and her whole face seems to give up. Like it's just *tired*.

"Mom?"

Candi shakes her head. "We've been scouring this mall for hours. My feet are killing me, and I'm starving." She turns to me. "Maybe you can call your contact and let him know what happened?"

I cringe a little. "He's sleeping?"

She sighs. "Let's get something to eat and regroup."

So we go inside Planet Hollywood, find a sandwich shop, and get some food. And even though it's almost three o'clock and I haven't seen Candi eat a bite all day, she orders her sandwich with no mayo and no cheese and gets a Diet Coke.

Heather has them hold "anything green," but I just tell them to load it up. A box of Oreos is not enough to power you through a day in Las Vegas, believe me!

As hungry as I am, it's still weird eating with Heather. Really unnatural. See, my lunchtime encounters with her at school are always stressful. Sometimes *painful*. Like the first day of seventh grade when I was sitting down eating my peanut butter and jelly sandwich and she came up out of the blue and jabbed me in my derriere with a pin.

Of course, after I'd gotten over the shock of what she'd done, I'd tracked her down and punched her in the nose, so it was actually more painful for *her,* but ever since that day I've been on guard when Heather's lurking near me at the lunch tables.

Anyway, we didn't say much as we ate, but we did eye each other a lot. So finally I just look straight at her and say, "I'm remembering a pin, what about you?"

"A broken nose," she says, and there's an angry glint in her eye.

I chuckle. "It wasn't broken, but you sure had everyone fooled with that big ol' cast you put over it." I glance back at her and ask what I've wondered since that first day of seventh grade. "Why'd you do it, anyway?"

She studies me a minute and finally says, "Because you think you're all that."

"I do not!"

She snorts. "Right."

"What's this about?" Candi asks.

"Never mind," Heather snaps.

But now Candi's looking at *me*, so I just shrug. "How I met your daughter?"

"Oh, that vicious welcome-to-junior-high-school punch in the nose?" Candi asks, and she's now looking very angry, too.

"Never *mind*," Heather says again, but as I look back and forth between Heather and her mother, the picture finally comes into focus. "No wonder you hate me," I tell Candi. "You don't know about the pin."

"What pin?" Candi demands.

"The pin she jabbed me with? The *reason* I punched her in the nose?"

"Never *mind*," Heather snaps again, and it's easy to see that I'm back on her kill list.

Candi looks at her daughter, then at me. So I put my hands up and say, "Sorry I brought it up."

Candi turns back to her daughter, and they have some fierce silent conversation before Candi finally says, "I think we should focus on why we're here." She hands me her phone. "Are you ready to make that call?"

"Maybe we should just go back to the Marriage Bureau?"

She considers me a minute. "Maybe you should first call your friend."

Now, I don't want to, but things are feeling really shaky, so I take the phone. And inside I'm cringing as the line is ringing, but Pete answers, sounding perky. "You've reached the King."

"Hey, I was afraid I'd wake you up!" Then I add, "It's Sammy."

"Well, hello, Miss Sammy. Normally I'd be in Dreamland, but it's lovers' weekend and Elvis is in big demand." Then he says, "So what's the good word?"

"We *almost* found her."

"Oooh. Too bad you ain't playin' horseshoes."

"No kidding. So now we'll probably go back over to the Marriage Bureau, but I was hoping you might get another tip."

He's quiet a second, then says, "It might help if you would ante up. I offered fifty bucks for a credible tip."

"You did?"

"Yeah, well, the Elvis Army likes to get paid. It's good motivation. And for you, I didn't mind. But I can't keep doin' that."

"Hang on a minute," I tell him, then look at Candi. "He paid fifty dollars for the last tip and wants to know if we'll put up fifty for the next one."

"What kind of friend is this?"

I shrug. "One with contacts who like to get paid?"

Heather butts in with "You're riding in our car, you're sleeping in our hotel room, and you're using our cell phones. . . . You're the one who should pay, not us."

Candi looks at her like, Good point! So I go back to the phone and say, "I'll put in the next fifty . . . and pay you back for the first."

"You sure?"

I thought about my reward money, shrinking fast in my pocket. "Yeah, I'm sure."

"I'm on it!" he says, and gets off the phone.

Heather's got a sharp eye on me. "How can you just throw a hundred dollars around like that? You always act like you're broke with your stupid peanut butter and jelly sandwiches and tacky torn-up jeans."

Candi hisses, "Heather!"

"Well, she does! I told you it's all just a big act!" Then she zooms in on her mother and says, "And stop hissing!"

Normally I would have explained about the reward money, but since Casey and I had worked *together* to get it and I knew Candi knew about his share, I'd be getting Casey in a whole lot of hot water if I said anything.

So instead I just say, "Think what you want, Heather, but I promise you, you haven't got a clue about my life. I'm just trying to get the job done." Then I turn to Candi and ask, "So are we going back to the Marriage Bureau?"

She looks at her watch. "It's already almost *four*? How late are they open?"

I shrug, but Heather gets online with her phone and says, "Midnight."

"Midnight?" Candi gasps. "Even on Saturdays?"

"Yup."

Candi blinks at her. "I don't want to stake out the Marriage Bureau until midnight!" But no one seems to have a better idea, so finally she says, "Okay, but first I've got to find the ladies' room."

"Me, too," Heather says.

So off we go in search of a bathroom, only as we're reading the overhead signs, I notice one that says CHAPEL with an arrow. "Hey!" I say, pointing to the sign. "Do you want to go look?" Then something hits me. "What if they're staying *here*? What if they're staying here and this is the chapel they're going to get married in! I mean, they were just strolling around the mall, right? Which is easy when you're staying in the resort that's connected to it, right? So what if they were just killing time until their wedding?"

We wind up going to the chapel, and even though it's locked up tight, we can peek inside, and I'm kinda shocked to see that the chapel is really *nice*.

Classy, even.

"Wow," I say, sort of to myself, "I actually *could* see Lady Lana getting married here."

"Lady Lana?" Heather asks.

I give a little shrug. "My nickname for my diva mother."

"You really don't like her, do you?" Candi asks.

I think about that a minute—about how the last time I

saw her, at Officer Borsch's wedding, I loved her to pieces for what she'd done to help Casey and me clear up an awful misunderstanding . . . but how quickly that had been overshadowed again by all the old hurt. And now that she'd delivered this new, hard slap in the face, sneaking off to marry my boyfriend's father without bothering to tell me, well, she was definitely back to being Lady Lana.

I sigh. "It's complicated."

Candi laughs. "Isn't it always?" Then she goes back to looking inside the chapel, even though we've seen all we need to see. And she *keeps* looking—just sort of gazing down the aisle—until finally I ask, "So what's next? Do you want to see if they're registered at the hotel?"

She sighs, then turns her back on the chapel. "What's next is the bathroom."

So we track down a bathroom, and I wait outside while the two of them go in to take care of business. Partly that's because I don't really need to use it, and partly that's because the girls' bathroom at school also holds stressful memories for me.

Let's just say you can't trust Heather to stay out of your stall.

Anyway, ten minutes later, I'm still waiting.

Fifteen minutes, still waiting.

And I'm thinking they're in there fixing their makeup or sneaking a smoke or just, you know, *stuck,* so I wait some more.

But finally I'm like, Come *on.* So I go inside, and guess what?

They're nowhere.

I check every stall, and then when I go into the vanity area, I discover that there's a second door—one that exits around the corner from where I'd been standing.

At first I can't believe that they're gone, so I check outside both doors and through the whole bathroom again, but they *are* gone, and really, there's only one way to explain it.

I've been ditched.

FIFTEEN

At first I couldn't believe it. And then I *still* couldn't believe it.

And then I got mad.

At Heather.

At her mother.

But mostly at me.

How could I have let Heather ditch me?

I guess I underestimated her. Or overestimated Candi. Of all things.

But there I was.

In Las Vegas.

Ditched.

I tried to keep the panic out of my brain, but that was kinda hard, seeing how I was all by myself in a huge city full of gamblers and drunks and strippers.

Think, I told myself. *Think*. Where could they be?

We'd talked about seeing if my mom and Warren had checked into the resort's hotel, so I ran, following signs through the casino and into the lobby.

The Ditchy Duo was nowhere.

So there I am, looking around, wondering why in the

world they ditched their only connection to new information, when all of a sudden it hits me.

Pete must've called while they were in the bathroom.

He must've called and they must've made a lucky guess and gotten a tip.

Just like that, I go from panicked to ticked off. And even though Heather and her mother could have been anywhere inside the Planet Hollywood complex or back inside the Miracle Mile Shops, what comes screeching into my brain is *Get to the car*. And yeah, maybe I should have found a pay phone and called Pete instead, but I'd already wasted a bunch of time and I didn't want Heather and Candi to get away. I mean, it was one thing to get ditched because they hated me. It was another to get ditched because they'd stolen my tip!

And the way I saw it, even if the tip was for somewhere inside the Miracle Mile or Planet Hollywood, eventually they'd go back to the car. And if they were leaving now, I'd never catch them once they drove away.

I had to get to the car!

Besides, it was something I could *do*. Something better than panicking about being all alone in a huge city with gamblers and drunks and strippers.

So I charge back through the casino and out to the Miracle Mile Shops, and even though I know Candi's feet are hurting her, those Acosta females are *determined*. I could just picture Candi hobbling along at lightning speed with popping blisters and oozing shoes while Heather's barking at her to hurry up.

And the more I play it through in my head, the more I realize that even if I run, I'll never catch them. They might have blistered feet and smokers' lungs, but they also have a *huge* head start.

But then I realize—I don't have to run.

I can ride!

I hop on my skateboard, knowing that mall security will kick me out . . . but I'm going out anyway, so who cares?

Besides, they'll have to catch me first!

There are shoppers everywhere, but I push along going, "Excuse me! Emergency! Coming through! Emergency!" and just like that, people are scampering out of my way. Pretty soon I'm picking up speed, weaving around planters and baby strollers, calling, "Sorry, emergency!" to people I startle and just flying down the shiny esplanade. And before any mall cop can shout, Stop that skater! I'm zipping out the doors that lead to the parking structure.

Now I can *really* power down, and I tear over to the elevator. But while I'm jabbing at the UP button, waiting for the doors to open, I hear something that makes me freeze.

Squealing tires.

Now, okay. Candi Acosta isn't the only crazy driver on the road. And maybe she isn't the one making a mad dash to escape, but somewhere on the echoey levels of the parking garage someone is definitely in a hurry to get out of there, and if it *is* Candi Acosta, there's only one thing for me to do.

Cut her off at the pass!

So I get back on my board and charge for the exit. And

since there's no guardrail or anything stopping cars from going in or out, I just hide behind a post near the exit ramp and try to catch my breath.

The squealing keeps going for another minute, and then there's a streak of red on my right.

As the car gets closer, I can see that it's definitely Candi and Heather. The windows are down and they've got one last turn to get into the exit ramp and out of the parking structure.

But the exit's a single lane, and I'm not going to let them out!

I step onto the ramp to block it, but when Candi sees me, she does something I wasn't expecting.

She starts to turn *away* from the ramp.

Like she's going to find another way out!

But all of a sudden Heather grabs the wheel and I can hear her screech, "She'll move!" and in a flash the car is veering right at me.

Candi's face looks totally panicked, and who knows what's wrong with her brake foot, but the car is not slowing down. And even though Heather's gambling with my *life*, she's right—I jump out of the way in the nick of time.

Candi still could stop, but she doesn't. Once I'm out of the way, she gets the car back on track and goes flying out of the parking structure and onto the street. And I do chase after them, but when they disappear around a corner, I know it's over. I mean, there's no way I'm going to be able to catch them, let alone follow them.

So I just stand there panting, and after a minute

everything that has happened comes crashing down and I feel like I've been slammed into a wall.

I'm just beat up.

Beat up and tired.

It's already dusky, and I have no idea what my next step should be. What I want more than anything is to collapse. My legs and arms are lead, and my heart is just *sagging* inside me, and for some reason finding my mother doesn't seem that important. I'm more worried about being on the streets of Las Vegas by myself with the sun going down and no place to stay.

It crosses my mind that I can go back to the MGM and wait outside Heather's door, but they'd nearly run me over just now trying to get rid of me, and once they'd found what they were looking for, there was no guarantee they'd spend another night there. And even if they did, I was pretty sure they wouldn't let me crash on their couch.

It's strange—I'd been in more dangerous situations before, but I hadn't felt *down* like this before. And as I'm riding along, I'm trying to put my finger on *why* I'm feeling so down. I mean, so Heather ditched me—so what? It's not like she was my friend or anything. And it's not like her knowing where my mom was and me not knowing was some big catastrophe. So she'd get there with Candi and mess up the wedding without me. So what? As long as *someone* put a monkey wrench in it, what did I care? I could corner Lady Lana about my dad . . . somewhere else.

But no matter how hard I tried, I couldn't seem to

reason my way out of feeling bad. It might not make *sense* to feel this way, but I still did. And what was weird was that the feeling *was* familiar.

A sort of déjà vu gut punch.

And that's when I realized that it was the same feeling I'd had when I first understood that my mother wasn't coming home. The feeling that someone's pulled out of your life and left you in a cloud of dust on the side of the road.

Being with Marissa and her mother and then Heather and Candi had distracted me from my fight with Grams. But now that was hitting me hard, too. Grams had gone along with my mother, my mother had left me behind, and there was nobody else in my family.

I was on the side of the road, totally abandoned.

I kept riding along, but I was having trouble breathing. My lungs felt pinched, my throat felt choked, and my eyes were stinging with tears. And all of a sudden, more than finding my mother or knowing who my father was or patching things up with Grams, what I wanted was to talk to Casey.

Casey.

Just the thought of him made me feel rescued. Not damsel-in-distress rescued—he was more like a light in the darkness. Someone who would help me find my way through all of this.

But as I headed down Las Vegas Boulevard looking for a pay phone to call him, I passed by a lady selling heart balloons and flowers, and another thought slugged me in the gut.

It was Valentine's Day!

I'd been so wrapped up in what I was doing that I hadn't even thought about how I was supposed to meet Casey at our secret spot for a picnic . . . and it was already dinnertime!

I told myself not to panic. I told myself he must've called Grams. Yes. He must've called Grams and found out that I was in Las Vegas.

But what if he hadn't?

What if he'd gone to the graveyard and I hadn't shown up and then he couldn't get a hold of Grams and . . . and . . . !

I felt so selfish and stupid. I mean, it's not like I'm in the habit of calling him anywhere but the high school pay phone, especially since his mother confiscated his cell phone. But the minute I knew his mother and sister were in Las Vegas, I should have called his house! I'd called half the wedding chapels in town and couldn't take a minute to call him?

Suddenly I was frantic to find a pay phone. I hurried down the Strip with my eyes peeled, asking random strangers if they knew where one was.

No one did.

One guy even said, "They still have those?"

And I was feeling so desperate that I wound up asking a skinny woman sitting cross-legged on the sidewalk with an accordion in her lap if she knew.

She looked up at me and her eyes seemed kind of wasted, but she pointed down the street and said, "There's one in the liquor store."

145

I just stared at her a minute, not knowing whether to believe her.

"Well, there is," she says, and starts playing some screechy notes on her accordion. And since there's a scarf with a sorry scattering of coins in front of her, I dig up two dollars, toss them in, and tell her, "Thanks!"

I find the liquor store no problem and go inside like I've got all the business in the world being there and spot the pay phone next to a rack of skanky magazines. And since I don't know how long it'll be before I get booted, I dial Casey's number quick and keep my back toward the register.

"Come on," I mutter after the fourth ring, but no one answers.

So I hang up quick before the voice recorder clicks on and eats my money, then I recycle the coins and try again.

And again.

And again.

Finally I give up and try Billy's number, and on the third ring I hear, "Yallo?"

"Billy!"

"Sammy-keyesta?"

"Yes—have you seen Casey?"

"Uh, negatory. I figured he'd be with you today."

"Oh, maaaaan!"

"What?"

"I'm an idiot."

He laughs. "Which is why we're friends!"

"I'm serious, Billy." I take a deep breath. "Look, if you hear from him—"

"Wait—you haven't seen him at *all*?"

"No. I . . . uh . . . I'm kinda outta town."

"Outta town? So he hasn't given you—" He clams up. "How far outta town?"

"Uh . . . would you believe Las Vegas?"

"*Nevada?*"

"Yeah. Nevada. It's a long story, okay? And I can't get into it other than to say Casey will know why I'm here. Is there any chance you can track him down and tell him I'm sorry?"

"Sure."

"Thank you! And I'll see you on Monday, okay?"

"You mean Tuesday!"

"Oh, right! I forgot we had a three-day weekend."

He laughs. "You *are* messed up, Sammy-keyesta!"

I laugh, too, and for one brief shining moment after we hang up, I feel happy.

That's the magic of Billy Pratt.

But two seconds later I'm feeling worse than ever. And after standing there with my gut in knots for a few minutes, I finally break down and call the one person I always seem to turn to when I'm in trouble.

Hudson.

Trouble is, he doesn't answer his phone, either.

And since *that* makes me feel even *worse*, I talk myself into calling Grams. I mean, I know I'm mad at her, but I also know she must be worried.

And that Casey for sure called her to find out where I was.

Trouble is, *she* doesn't answer the phone, *either*.

147

So, great.

I've totally struck out.

I try to forget about neglecting Casey and being abandoned and force myself to get back on track. I dig up Pete's number, but after four rings it rolls over to voice mail. And I'm sure not going to hang around a skanky liquor store waiting for him to call me back, so I don't leave the number. I just hang up. But then I start thinking that maybe he's in a busy place and didn't hear his phone, so I try again.

And again.

And finally I give up and decide to check back at the place where I'd found him the night before. So I leave the liquor store and trudge up the street past the accordion lady and Planet Hollywood and what feels like miles of people to Paris Las Vegas and around the bend.

Too bad for me, the Elvises have left the sidewalk.

"Maaaaaan!" I cry, and now I really *am* panicking. The city lights are up, the sun is down, and I have no idea where to turn, who to call, or what to do.

SIXTEEN

I don't know what I was thinking.

Well, actually I do.

I was thinking that I could cruise the streets of Las Vegas and find Elvis.

Smart, huh? But since I couldn't reach Pete by phone, and since he was the only possible connection to either Candi and Heather or my mother, I had to try.

I rode my skateboard whenever I could, keeping my eyes peeled for Elvises of any kind. Big ones, mini ones . . . If there really was an Elvis Army, any of them might know where Pete was and why he wasn't answering his phone.

But the Strip seemed to go on forever, and the farther I went, the fewer people there were out walking, which was good for riding, but when what I was riding through was pretty much just trashy women and bums, I started wishing for more people, not less.

Construction forced me to cross the street, and when I came to a place called Circus Circus, it *really* felt like I'd hit the dregs. Where the rest of the Strip was flashy and huge and *tall*, Circus Circus was a building in the shape of a red-and-white big top tent and looked like it had been there forever. Also, instead of fancy fountains or statues or palm trees like the other places had, Circus Circus had a lot of cement, and next to it was a weedy lot surrounded by chain-link fencing. I half expected to see a sad, lonely elephant with a big headdress in the lot, but it was pretty shadowy and all I could see was broken bottles and a bunch of shriveled-up weeds.

Now, not only do I have bad history with places that have chain-link fencing and shriveled-up weeds, I really didn't think Elvis would be hanging around a vacant elephant yard. So I finally turned around and started back the way I'd come.

It's funny how you can space out when you're riding a skateboard. Well, unless you're really *moving*, and then you've got to concentrate. But since I was already familiar with the route, and since the sidewalks at this end were pretty open, I wound up riding along on autopilot. And pretty soon I'm back to thinking about how I'd been ditched.

Me!

Ditched!

And by a *mother*.

What kind of mother ditches a thirteen-year-old, let alone in Vegas? It didn't matter that I was her daughter's archenemy. She'd stolen my tip—well, that was the only thing that made sense—and then abandoned a thirteen-year-old, one who'd been very polite and helpful, especially considering the snotty way her daughter had acted, and left her to fend for herself in a town full of gamblers and drunks and strippers!

Not that me being safe was *her* problem, but come on! We were supposed to be working together!

Now, yesterday I would have expected this. But I really thought we'd made some progress. Candi had been pretty normal—especially considering that until this Vegas trip, she'd always come at me like a rabid hissing cat. And Heather *had* gone a whole half hour without calling me loser.

But after I'd mentioned the pin, things had apparently reset to pre-Vegas. Probably because Heather was afraid I would say other things that would knock a hole in the wall of lies she'd built up about me.

What's funny is, before sitting down to eat with Heather, I hadn't thought about the pin jab in ages. It had happened over a year ago, and she'd done a bunch of way more vicious things since then, so the jab had sort of faded in my mind.

But now I was thinking about it again, wondering why in the world she'd done it in the first place. I mean, a person doesn't just go off and jab another person with a pin because they won't give them some lunch money. It wasn't like a stick-'em-up where she said, Give me money or I jab you! It was more like a stick-and-*run* where I'd already said no and she'd used that as an *excuse* to jab me.

So as I'm rolling down the Strip, I rewind to that morning when we first met. Heather had been talking to an eighth-grade guy named Taylor when Marissa and I had stepped up to ask for help finding our homeroom. And although Heather had snubbed us and made a crack about my high-tops, Taylor had been friendly and helpful, which had totally backcombed Heather.

I didn't get it, that's for sure. It's not like we were flirting with Taylor. We were just sort of nervous and lost. But it seemed to flick some possessive switch in Heather's brain, and before you know it, she's jabbing me with a pin and I'm punching her in the nose.

After that she became Psycho Heather, constantly looking for a way to get back at me. I always said it was because she didn't like my shoes, since I really couldn't explain how she could be so bent out of shape over a war she'd started.

But now the picture of Heather and her dad flashed through my mind, and for the first time I could see that the road through Heather's Valley of Hatred started *before* I stumbled onto it. That there were signposts *behind* Taylor's Gulch or the Cliffs of Casey. Signs I hadn't seen before, because I'd entered the valley from a side road and had concentrated on getting *out* instead of looking back.

"Wow," I gasped, because as I looked back through the valley now, there was a giant flashing neon sign that was impossible to miss.

WARREN'S EXIT.

The girl in the picture with Warren was not the girl I knew. She was carefree and *happy*. And knowing Heather now, there was something really . . . *sad* about seeing how she used to be. And as I rode along picturing her with that sunny smile and her arms wrapped around her father's neck, it hit me that maybe that's where it all came from.

From trying to hold on.

From being forced to let go.

From feeling left behind.

Abandoned.

That thought actually knocked me off my skateboard and made me pull over. It's like I couldn't even hold it in my head, let alone ride a skateboard or even *walk* with it echoing around up there.

Whatever had happened between Candi and Warren, Warren had left, and Heather had been left behind.

Sort of like Lady Lana had left me behind.

And it wasn't that Warren had actually *abandoned* Heather, but people would say the same thing about my mom. Lady Lana checks in, "tries to communicate," and sometimes actually visits. And *she* would say that at least half our problems come from me being "disengaged" or "antagonistic" or just plain "bratty"—words I'd have no problem using to describe Heather.

I tell you, when you find some deep connection between you and your archenemy, it is scary stuff. And really, I didn't know what to do with this little revelation. I'd had a pang of sympathy for Heather when I'd seen the picture of her and her dad, but now?

This was worse than a pang of sympathy.

This was us in the same boat.

Us rowing with only one oar.

Us trying not to drown in our little oceans of hurt feelings . . . which had somehow merged into one gigantic ocean of mixed-up hurt feelings.

I was back in the busy part of the Strip now, so I just

stood off to the side, blinking and thinking and wanting to go back to not having made this connection. I mean, this made things so *complicated*. It was much easier when Heather was simply psycho.

After trying to make sense of everything flashing through my brain, I found myself wanting to *talk* to Heather.

Crazy, I know!

I mean, for one thing, she wouldn't listen. She'd call me a loser and shut me down before I could get out what I wanted to say.

And . . . I didn't really *know* what I wanted to say.

There was so much Heather didn't know about me. And she wouldn't believe I really understood her situation unless she did know. But I couldn't tell her anything without risking everything. If she ratted me and Grams out, we'd be kicked out of the Highrise, and Grams couldn't afford to live anywhere else.

And how could I risk that—*why* would I risk that—just to patch together some sort of peace with Heather?

A peace she would probably just reject anyway.

My brain felt really muddled, and I stood there for the longest time, trying to sort things out. And even though part of me kept reminding the *other* part of me that I'd been *ditched in Las Vegas* by Heather and her mother, my new little revelation kept getting in the way of being totally ticked off.

Which ticked the first part of me off big-time!

I mean, come on!

I'd been ditched in Sin City!

Finally I started down the Strip again. I was obviously getting nowhere standing around thinking, and since I was having zero luck tracking down any Elvises, I wanted to get back to the pay phone and try calling Pete again.

And maybe Grams.

And Hudson.

And definitely Casey.

Because even riding my skateboard couldn't keep that panicky feeling from bubbling up again. It was now dark, I was exhausted, and I had no plan.

I did keep my eyes peeled for other pay phones, but I didn't see any, so I eventually wound up back at the liquor store.

The guy behind the counter was busy watching his surveillance monitor, so I slipped over to the pay phone, and the first thing I did was call Casey. I just wanted to *talk* to someone, you know? And Casey was my number one choice.

There was no answer, though, so I tried Hudson.

No answer there, either, so I stared at the phone for a long time and decided not to call Grams. I wasn't really *as* mad at her anymore—not that I knew why—but it seemed kind of heartless to call her and tell her what was going on. It was better for her to think I was mad at her and in Las Vegas with Marissa and her mother than to know the truth.

I also thought about calling Marissa, because she had to be home by now, only that felt selfish. She had plenty of worries of her own without me piling on, and besides, if she wasn't home dealing with McKenze madness, she was probably getting ready to escape to the Valentine's dance with the rest of my friends.

So I skipped Grams and Marissa and called Elvis. And after the second ring, I about jumped for joy when I heard, "You've reached the King!"

"Pete!"

"Who's this?"

"Sammy!"

He hesitates. "You're not calling from the usual number."

"Yeah, well, I've been ditched. I'm guessing they tricked a tip out of you."

"Tricked a—well, that would explain why you stood me up."

"I stood you up?"

"I waited for you in front of the Hard Rock like we agreed. You were gonna square up for the tips. I was booked to do an appearance at a party, so I couldn't wait around forever, but when you didn't show up and didn't answer your phone, I figured you'd gotten what you wanted and stiffed me."

"No! And it wasn't me you talked to. I have no idea what the tip was or where they went, but I promise to pay you, okay?"

He's quiet a second, then says, "*Why* are you workin' with these people?"

I let out a big sigh. "It's too long and complicated to explain. Can you just tell me what you told them? And then tell me where I can meet up with you to pay you?"

"Well, here's the deal. That tip I got a few hours ago was for Mandalay Bay."

"The big place across from the airport?"

"Exactly! She was spotted on the first floor, going into the House of Blues."

I didn't really know what the House of Blues was, but it didn't seem to matter. "She's gotta be long gone by now."

"You could check out the casino. People get caught up gamblin', you know."

"But . . . she's not here to gamble, she's here to get married!"

"Hmmm," he says.

That's all.

Just "Hmmm."

"What are you saying?"

"I've seen a lot of brides, Sammy. She's not acting like one. She's not dressed like one. You sure that's why she's here?"

"Yes! And what do you mean, she's not acting like one and she's not dressed like one?"

I can practically see him shrug. "Brides go to the spa. Have a manicure. Get their hair done. Shop."

"She *was* shopping!"

"But she didn't *buy.* She's not carrying bags in either picture."

"Wait. What pictures?"

"You think I'm gonna hand out fifties with no proof? I got two picture texts—both are her."

"Can I see them?" Then I add, "I have to square up with you anyway, right?"

"That'd be nice, sure." He thinks a minute. "How about I meet you at the House of Blues."

"Uh . . . I go to Mandalay Bay and go inside?"

"Yeah. It's on the first floor. Let's meet at the box office. I'm at the Excalibur right now, so it's not too far for me, and you'll be headin' there anyway, right?"

"Got nowhere better to go."

"So where are you right now?"

"Uh . . . inside a liquor store somewhere between that big Paris balloon and the MGM."

"You're . . . Sammy, get the hell out of there. What are you doing in that dive?"

"It's the only pay phone I could find!"

"Well, hang it up and get out!" Then he adds, "It'll take you a while to get to Mandalay Bay, so I'm going to work the streets a little, okay? But I'll be there, all right?"

"So will I, promise."

Then I head out, glad that I found at least one person to talk to.

Even if it's an Elvis impersonator.

And I owe him a hundred bucks.

SEVENTEEN

So much about Las Vegas feels like an illusion. Or maybe it's just a real-life study in perspective. Whatever. I rode and I rode and I rode and was really relieved to *finally* get past the big pyramid. But then it was another forever of riding to get to the Mandalay Bay walkway, and then *another* endless ride past huge waterfalls and little lakes and palm trees galore to get to the actual entrance.

Anyway, what I find inside is a resort like the MGM Grand, only grander. And *golder*. Definitely not meant for a ragamuffin girl and her skateboard.

Still, I try to walk like I *do* belong and know exactly where I'm going as I make my way through the Hundred-Acre Lobby. And I figure if this place is anything like the MGM, the thing to do is get to the casino, where there'll be handy-dandy signs hanging overhead telling me which way to go to get to the House of Blues.

The trouble with acting like you know where you're going is that it requires speed. You don't meander if you know where you're going. You don't wander or saunter or, you know, *dawdle*. But walking like you know where you're going when you *don't* can be really embarrassing if

159

you wind up at a dead end and have to make a U-turn. I mean, you still have to *act* like you went that way on purpose, when anyone watching knows you're completely lost in a maze of slot machines and poker tables.

But part of the reason I keep having to make U-turns is that there are no signs for the House of Blues. Anywhere! Plus I don't know what the House of Blues looks like. I'd heard it's a music place. And I *figure* it's in the shape of a house and that there'll be, you know, *blueness* involved. So when I finally find it, I'm like, Really? I mean, the only way I can tell it's the House of Blues is that there's a flaming red heart above the entrance with HOUSE OF BLUES over it. Which, trust me, should say HOUSE OF MUD instead.

Seriously, the place looks like a big mud cave with a gazillion chunks of . . . *stuff* embedded in the walls. Colored glass, pieces of metal, smooth stones, little *masks* . . . It's the weirdest place I've ever seen, and there's absolutely nothing blue about it.

Anyway, I guess I'm gawking because a guy with gauges in his ears and full-sleeve tattoos grins at me as he heads inside. "Cool, huh?"

What's funny is, I'm actually relieved to see a scary-looking guy with gauges and tattoos 'cause he's the first person I've seen in the resort who looks like he doesn't belong there, either. So I nod and say, "I've never seen anything like it."

"Outsider art," he tells me, then gives me one of those cool-guy head jerks that means "See ya" and cruises inside.

I step forward a few feet, but what I see is not a music

place, it's a restaurant. One that looks like it's been plucked out of a bayou. It's got a huge tree in the middle of the room, lots of strings of lights, and a whole swampy vibe.

So if the House of Blues is a swampy restaurant inside a mud cave . . . why would there be a box office?

A waitress with an empty drink tray sees me gawking and calls over, "May I help you?"

"Is there a box office?" I ask her.

She points back out and to my left. "Just around the corner."

"So you're a restaurant and . . . what?"

"A concert hall?" she says, like she's not sure I could really be asking such an obvious question. Then she adds, "We're also a gift shop."

"Oh." Then real quick I say, "Uh, have you maybe seen"—I dig up my mom's picture—"this person?"

She comes over and checks out the picture. "No," she says, shaking her head.

"You sure?"

"Pretty sure, yeah."

"When did your shift start?"

"At three."

So since I can't think of anything else to ask, I just tell her thanks and head around the corner the way she'd pointed.

I don't see any box office, but I do see the gift shop. It's another big cave entrance with weird art all over it, and when I go inside, I see it's full of House of Blues T-shirts and rock 'n' roll groupie stuff.

Well, Lady Lana wouldn't be caught dead in here, but the guy behind the register isn't busy, so I go up and show him her pictures anyway.

"Don't remember her," he says.

So I ask him, "Where's the box office?" and he points back out the door and says, "Just around the corner."

So I go back out and keep going, and sure enough, there's a box office.

The first thing I notice is that there's no Elvis hanging around.

The second thing I notice is the marquee. It lists six dates, and next to February 14 is DARREN COLE—SOLD OUT.

Just like that, I feel miserable. I mean, talk about whiplash karma. I'm standing at the place where Darren Cole—the guy who wrote Casey's and my song—is playing on Valentine's Day?

And like someone going, Tisk-tisk-tisk! right in front of me is a picture of ol' Darren with his arms crossed, looking tough in front of his band of Troublemakers.

Suddenly all I want to do is call Casey. So I go up to the box office and ask the guy inside, "Is there a pay phone nearby?"

"Right around the corner," he says, pointing.

So I continue going "right around the corner" but all I see are escalators next to a mini food court. So I *keep* going and what I find as I enter the mini food court is *not* a pay phone.

It's also not Elvis.

It's the Queen of the Ditch.

The Mama Witch.

The one and only Candi Acosta.

Now, back in Santa Martina I'd have thrown myself in reverse and gotten out of there quick. But here all I can think about is how I've been ditched in Sin City by this woman, and for some reason that thought changes everything.

She's not scary anymore.

She's pathetic.

Well, she's also a liar and a sneak and a thief and a coward, but what that adds up to is pathetic. Plus, she's not *looking* very scary. She's sitting in a bistro chair with her shoes off, her hands wrapped around a paper coffee cup, and her eyes closed.

I look around for Heather, and when I don't see her anywhere, I sneak up to Candi's table, slip into the chair across from her, lean forward so my face is pretty close to hers, and thump my skateboard on the ground hard to wake her up.

Her eyes fly open, her cup knocks over, and all of a sudden she's face to face with me. "Aaaah!" she cries, and practically falls backward trying to get away from me.

"You must be so proud," I tell her, "ditching a thirteen-year-old."

If this had been Heather, she would have called me a name and made some snide remark. Or jabbed me with a pin. And since Candi seems like she's just a grown-up version of Heather, I'm expecting her to do something similar.

So I about fall out of *my* chair when her face crinkles up and she says, "Oh, Sammy! I'm so relieved to see you! I've been feeling terrible! I can't believe . . . I can't believe any of this!"

I just sit there sort of mentally shaking out my ears, and finally I squint and say, "She *would* have killed me, you know."

"She knew you would move!" Even to her this sounds totally lame, so right away she covers her face and says, "I couldn't believe it. I still can't believe it." She drops her hands. "And then I just left you behind! How could I do that? Why do I listen to her?" She shakes her head hard and fast. "I can't control her anymore! She's . . . she's . . . I don't know what to do!"

I lean back a little and snort. "Boy. I know how you feel."

Then she surprises me again by saying, "I want to know the story of the pin. All I can get out of her is that you're a liar." She searches my face. "But if you're lying, her reaction doesn't make sense!" She shakes her head. "But her jabbing you doesn't make sense, either! Why would she do that?"

I study her a minute, then say, "I think it had to do with Marissa and me interrupting a conversation she was having with an eighth-grade boy named Taylor."

"She jabbed you for interrupting a conversation?"

"It was the first day of seventh grade and Marissa and I were lost, so we went up and asked them where our home-room was. Heather snubbed us, but Taylor was friendly and helped us out."

She frowns a little. "Damsels in distress."

"We didn't think so, but I think *she* did, because later

in homeroom she started sneering at me and making fun of me, and the teacher embarrassed her in front of the class . . . which she probably blamed on me. So she came up to Marissa and me at lunch and asked for lunch money—"

"But she has her own lunch money!"

"I'm just telling you what happened. You don't have to believe it if you don't want to, but you asked. And she probably only asked for money because Marissa's family used to be rich and—"

"Used to be?"

I shake my head. "Long story. But bottom line, Heather asked for money, and when we turned her down, she jabbed me with a pin—which really hurt, by the way—so I punched her in the nose." I let out a puffy-cheeked sigh. "And that's how it all started."

She takes a super deep breath, then shakes her head, saying, "Cute, rich damsels in distress."

"I'm not rich!"

Her eyebrows go flying. "You'll pay fifty dollars for a tip without blinking an eye?"

"No! I—"

"It's okay," she says, putting up a hand. "It's just that it's been a struggle for us, you know? Heather's very . . . resentful of people who are in a better position than we are."

"But I—"

"She's also very style-conscious, which is expensive, but I think it's important for a girl to . . . to develop confidence." She eyes me. "Obviously you already have that."

My eyes go a little buggy. "Because of how I dress?"

She gives me a sort of sad smile. "Everything about you says confidence." She looks at me eye to eye for the longest time until finally she says, "But you're not at all what I expected."

"Neither are you," I tell her, and at that moment it's true—never in a million years did I think I'd have a conversation like this with Candi Acosta. Then I look around and ask, "Where is Heather, anyway?"

She tosses a hand in the air. "Searching for her father. I just let her go." She sighs. "You've got to be able to admit when it's over."

I study her. "But it's not over. What I said before about you and him is true, isn't it?"

She looks at me. Looks down. Looks at me. Looks down.

"Why can't you admit it?"

Her face crinkles up and she blurts out, "Yes, I still love him." Then right away she covers her face. "I can't believe I just said that."

"So he doesn't know?"

"He thinks I hate him. And I thought I did! I don't know . . . everything just . . . escalated."

"Into a divorce?"

"Yes!"

"But you don't want to be divorced?"

"No! I wish we could just . . . erase all the hurt. I wish we could find a way. . . ."

She just trails off, so I finally ask, "Is there any chance *he* still loves *you*?"

"With your mother in the picture?" Her eyes spring full of tears. "I don't have a chance."

"But he did love you at some point. And you have two kids together?"

She blots away a tear and shakes her head like there's no way things could ever go back to that.

"Look," I tell her. "You probably think I'm talking about this because I don't want him to marry my mom, but . . ."

"But what?"

I let out a big sigh. "I went clear up to Circus Circus and clear back down here. It was a *long* way to ride, but it gave me a long time to think about your family, about my family . . . about everything." I kind of tilt my head and ask, "When you split up, how did Heather wind up living with you, and Casey with Warren?"

"That's just how we divided things."

I stare at her 'cause it sounds like she's talking about property.

She must have thought so, too, because she hurries to say, "That sounds terrible, I know, but the kids weren't getting along, either." She shrugs. "It just made sense."

I let this sink in for a minute, then ask, "Have you seen that picture Heather has on her phone?" I quickly add, "The one of her and her dad?" because I know of some pictures on Heather's phone that no mother would want to see.

She shakes her head. "She won't let me touch her phone."

"Well, you need to see that picture for this to make sense, but what I came up with on my ride over here is that maybe Heather felt like her dad chose Casey over her."

"*What?*"

"Maybe it made her mad and then insecure. Especially about guys choosing someone else over her. Which is why she got so bent out of shape about Taylor that first day of school."

"But . . . Warren didn't *choose* Casey—we thought it was better for a boy to be with his dad and a girl to be with her mom!"

"But I don't think that's how Heather feels about it. Or felt about it. She was ten, right? Something like that?"

"Eleven."

"So maybe it made *sense* to split your kids up like that, but it hurts to feel left behind."

For some reason saying this puts a lump in my throat. And what I should have done was not say anything else, but all of a sudden it's like I *need* to say it. "It really *hurts,*" I tell her, and this time tears are stinging my eyes.

"But she wasn't left behind! Warren's been . . . involved. And I've worked really hard to give her a good home!"

"Look, Heather acts tough, but maybe that's because she's hurt. Someone, something, the *situation* came between her and Warren and maybe *that's* what she hates, but since there's nothing she can do about it, she takes it out on other people."

The more I talk about this, the more my throat closes up, and I know I should just stop talking. But deep down inside it feels like I'm gasping for air—like my *heart* is gasping for air—and that the only way I'll be able to breathe again is to finish what I'm trying to say. So I choke out, "I know it hurts, 'cause my mother chose being a movie star over being my mom. It's not the same thing, but now that Warren's moved down to L.A., it's close, and it makes you feel unwanted and unloved and . . . and . . . *abandoned*."

And there I am, crying in front of Candi Acosta.

Candi Acosta!

"But . . . what about your dad?" she asks, reaching for my hand. "Doesn't he make you feel wanted and secure?"

And I don't know—maybe it was the stress from the whole trip to Las Vegas. But at this point I'm completely exhausted and hysterical, and she's holding my *hand,* and before I know what I'm saying, I blurt out, "I don't even know who he is!"

Her jaw drops. "You . . ."

And just then Heather swoops in with "What the hell is going on?" And let me tell you, her eyes are on *fire.*

I yank back my hand and try to hide the fact that I've been crying. "Nothing," I tell her. Then I pick up my skateboard and whisper to Candi, "Find him and tell him how you feel."

Candi just stares, but Heather chases after me. "What was that about? Hey! Where are you going?"

"What do you care?" I grumble.

She follows me, demanding, "What were you saying to my mother?"

"We were discussing traffic laws and what kind of jail time you'd serve for running down kids in the road." I pick up the pace because I'm panicked over what I've just told Candi. Besides the whole well-who-*does*-she-live-with? problem, once Candi told Heather what I'd said, things would get *brutal* at school. Talk about giving your arch-enemy an arsenal of ammo! What kind of an idiot was I?

But as much as I want to get away from her, Heather stays on my tail. "What did you really tell her?" she demands, and when I don't say anything, she grabs my arm and shouts, "Tell me!"

I yank my arm away and keep walking, but then it hits me that *she's* worried. Worried that I might have told her mother all sorts of things. Not just about what she's done to me, but about things like her circulating racy pictures of herself with older guys. Or the fact that she smokes. Or about what really happened to her cell phone that disappeared. Or . . . wow, there were so many things!

And I'm actually thinking that maybe I could find some way to put *Heather* in the hot seat . . .

But then we turn the corner.

EIGHTEEN

In the time I'd been around the corner talking to Candi, a
line had formed outside the House of Blues and was running through the big open area between the box office and
into the casino. And standing in a group between the line
and us are four Elvises.

This is even weirder than seeing Pete on the Strip with
the first group of impersonators, because not only are these
Elvi all wearing the same white outfit, they're all about the
same size. It's like seeing Elvis in some weird fractured universe. Or a kaleidoscope. Or the mirrored stairwell at the
Heavenly Hotel.

"Sammy!" Pete calls, waving real big.

Which kind of messes with my fractured universe thing
because none of the other Elvi's arms go up.

"Who's *that*?" Heather asks.

I raise an eyebrow her way. "Elvis Presley?"

"No, stupid, who's he really?"

I stop cold. "You know what? I don't need to put up
with you. After what you did? You can take your bad atti-
tude and run people over with it all around town, but stay
away from me."

But she's already figured it out. "That's your *connection*?" she laughs. "Your source is a wannabe *Elvis*?"

"It's the entire Elvis Army," I growl at her. "And they're here to get paid, so unless you've got fifty bucks for the tip you stole, back off."

That does make her *hesitate,* but she doesn't leave. "You shouldn't pay them. Their tips were bogus."

"That's her?" one of the other Elvises says to Pete. "She's just a kid."

"But she's got one really hot mama," another one says.

"Knock it off!" Pete tells him. He steps closer to us and eyes Heather. "I'm guessin' this is the sneak who tricked me."

"Yup, that's her," I tell him. "Stole a tip, tried to run me over with her mother's car, ditched me . . . The list of crimes goes on and on."

The Army has also advanced. "So you two are sisters?" one of the Elvises asks.

"No!" Heather and I say, looking at each other with wide eyes.

Elvis shrugs. "That's the kind of stuff *my* sisters did to each other."

"Mine, too," the Elvis next to him says with a nod.

"Give us some space, would you?" Pete tells them. "Give us some space and I'll get you your money."

"Right, right," the Army says, and when they've retreated, Pete whips out his phone.

I look at Heather. "I said back off. If you're not paying, you don't get to see. I'm done being stabbed in the back by you."

"You're just sore because—"

"Back off!"

She does step back, and I pull Pete even farther away, saying, "She really did try to run me over."

He eyes her again. "One of these days you're going to have to explain this whole deal to me." Then he scrolls through his phone and brings up a picture.

And there she is.

Beautiful as ever.

My mother.

It's a picture of just her, and I recognize the Miracle Mile Shops behind her, but Pete was right—she's carrying no bags. Plus her purse is tiny. "Yeah, that's her," I tell him.

"Here's the other one," he says as he taps on his phone.

And there she is again, this time up close and with a surprised look on her face. Like some rogue Elvis jumped out of nowhere and snapped a picture.

Warren's partly in the picture, too. It's just his shoulder, but it's definitely a maroon leather jacket with fringe. It's hard to tell the background, though, so I ask, "Where was this one taken?"

"Hey, Chewy!" Pete calls over to the Elvises. "Where'd you get this shot?"

"Right over there!" Chewy-Elvis says, pointing toward the escalators.

"Going up or down?" I call.

"They came down and went inside the House of Blues." Then he adds, "Any chance we could move this along? The night's not getting any younger!"

"Yeah," another Elvis calls. "I need to boogie or Benny and me'll get towed!"

"Sorry," Pete says to me, 'cause he knows I'm looking at a picture that's over three hours old and am having to pay a hundred bucks for basically nothing. "I tried. And really, I'll split it with you."

"That's okay." I dig up a hundred bucks and hand it over. "It was nice of you to help me out. I guess it was stupid to think I could find her in this crazy place."

He takes the money and shakes his head. " 'Crazy' doesn't even begin to describe it."

"Does that mean you miss Santa Martina?"

"No!" he says with a laugh. "It's good to be gone." Then he nods over my shoulder and says, "At least you're not here alone."

I look behind me and there's Candi, her shoes gripped in one hand and her daughter's arm gripped in the other— which explains why Heather hadn't swooped back in when I was looking at the pictures.

"You gonna be okay with them?" Pete asks as he heads toward the Elvis Army with my cash. "Got a place to stay and all?"

"I'll be fine," I tell him, 'cause what else am I going to say? Uh, no. Can I crash on your couch?

But Candi must've heard because she calls, "She'll be fine. She's staying with us."

"Mom, no!" Heather cries.

"She's staying with us!" Candi tells her. "And we're going to have a big, long talk tonight."

"No!" Heather wails. It's a desperate wail, too. Like she thinks I've given her mother all sorts of dirt on her.

"Maybe I'll just try to get a flight home," I tell Candi.

"No! You're staying with us. And if we haven't made any progress by tomorrow, you can get a ride home with us, too."

"Mom!" Heather cries. "Why are you *punishing* me? What did she tell you?" She gives me a desperate look, then turns back to her mother and blurts out, "Whatever she told you, I can explain! I can explain everything!"

"My," Candi says, studying her daughter. "This gets more interesting by the minute." She arches an eyebrow at her. "Sammy actually said some remarkably *understanding* things about you."

First Heather's face goes blank, then her eyes go shifty. "She did?"

"Mm-hmm."

"Great to see ya, Sammy!" Pete calls as the Army starts to scatter. "Should I use that same number if somethin' comes up?"

"Sure," I call back.

"Any tip from me is free, of course!" Then he says, "Hey, Eddie, where are you and Benny parked?"

"At the Blues loading dock—if I haven't already been towed!"

Pete hurries after them. "Where you headed?"

"Up to Bally's."

"Can you drop me at the Monte Carlo?"

"And me at the Marketplace?" Chewy-Elvis calls.

"As long as you bums promise to get out!" Eddie-Elvis tells them.

There's a chorus of Elvis laughter and then off they go past the House of Blues and out of sight.

When they're gone, Candi comes closer, saying, "Are we calling it a night?"

I turn to face her. "Thanks for offering to let me stay."

She nods. "I don't know about the two of you, but I'm exhausted. And we've been here for hours, so"—she shrugs—"we need to face facts. They're long gone, and we have no idea where to look."

"I can't believe this," Heather grumbles.

Well, obviously what she can't believe is not that we haven't found my mom and her dad—it's that she hasn't been able to get rid of me. But I ignore her and tell Candi, "I'm all out of ideas, too."

"So let's call it a night."

But as we're walking past the House of Blues restaurant, I catch a glimpse of something that makes me do a double take.

"Sammy?" Candi asks, because I'm moving away from them fast.

I say, "Hang on!" over my shoulder as I hurry into the restaurant, and sure enough, there's a man in a fringed maroon leather jacket. I call, "Warren!" because he's clear across the restaurant and walking away, and when he doesn't hear me, I shout out, "Hey, Warren!"

He doesn't turn around, though, and in a flash Heather is next to me, going, "Where?"

"He went down that hallway!"

We hurry over and discover that the hallway is actually more like a tunnel. It has a floor that slants down between painted red walls, and a few yards ahead of us there's a velvet rope, which definitely means keep out.

There are no side doors that I can see, and since the tunnel turns right just past the velvet rope, Heather's dad could only have gone one way.

"Come on!" I tell Heather, and duck under the rope.

"Are you sure it was him?" Heather whispers as she follows along.

But before I can answer, we hear, "Hey! Hey-hey-hey!" from behind us, and sure enough, we're busted.

Now, if I'd known where I was going, I might have just made a break for it, but what I see around the corner is a longer tunnel, which leads into something dark and cave-like. And since the guy busting us is as big as a gorilla, I stop and face him and try and explain. "Her dad just went through here and we're trying to—"

He grabs each of us by the arm. "Sure you are."

"No, seriously! Her dad was—"

"No, seriously," he growls, hauling us back around the rope, "I've heard it all before."

"But we've been trying to find him all day!"

He gives me a meaty grin. "I'm sure you have."

"Please! He's the guy in the fringed jacket. Just tell him his daughter is here and looking for him."

His grin grows into a gap-toothed smile. "Oh, he'll

love that. I'm sure he'll run right out to see you." And before I can say anything else, he tosses us back into the restaurant so hard we catch air. "Next time I won't be so gentle," he growls, then turns and lumbers back down to the cave.

NINETEEN

"Are you sure it was him?" Heather asks after we pick our-selves up.

"Would I go in there if I wasn't?"

"Yes!"

I study her a minute, and out of my mouth comes "Good point."

And I don't know—something about it makes me laugh.

And something about *me* laughing makes *her* laugh. "Am I right, or what?"

"Just this once, though!" I tell her.

Now, let me tell you, having a laugh with your arch-enemy is a pretty confusing thing for your mind to pro-cess. Any other thoughts that may be churning away in the background of your brain are completely overshadowed by the fact that you're laughing with someone you hate.

So it took longer than it should have for me to rec-ognize that the answer to Heather's question was no. I *wasn't* sure, because I hadn't actually seen her dad's face. It was definitely the right jacket, and the hair color was right, but . . .

"When's the last time you saw your dad?"

Heather blinks at me a minute.

Like *her* brain *also* can't quite process that she was laughing with her archenemy.

Finally she says, "Uh . . . it's been a while."

"Is his hair still short?"

"I think. That's how it's been on *Lords*." Then she catches on. "Wait—the guy we were chasing had *long* hair?"

"It wasn't *long* . . . but it was a little shaggy."

"So it *wasn't* my dad?"

"The jacket was definitely maroon with fringe."

"There's probably a hundred jackets just like that in Vegas!"

"The lady at the mall said she'd never seen one like it."

"So? What does she know? She sells *jewelry*."

"But one of Pete's pictures had the arm of a jacket in it."

"Pete? Who's Pete?"

"You know, Elvis?"

"Oh." She thinks a minute. "Just the arm of the jacket?"

"The rest of your dad was cut off but his arm was in. And it was definitely that same jacket!"

"Why was he cut off?"

"Because they were looking for my mom, not your dad."

"Why weren't they looking for my dad, too?"

"Because they only had a picture of my mom!"

"But I could have sent him the picture of my dad!"

"Except you were too busy ditching me to think of that, right?"

"Girls!" Candi cries. "I've been looking all over for you. What is going on?"

"What's Dad's hair look like?" Heather demands.

"What?"

"His hair! Has he changed it?"

"Not that I know of." She looks back and forth at us. "Did you *see* him?"

"I think so," I tell her. "I saw a man with his color hair wearing a fringed maroon jacket. But he went around the corner before I could see his face."

"But the Elvises said that he and your mom came in here, right?" Candi says. "They had a picture and everything, right?"

I shake my head a little. "I know, but that was three or four hours ago. And when I showed a waitress the picture of my mom, she didn't recognize her."

Candi's eyes are getting wider and wider. "But it must be him! Two distinctive fringed maroon jackets are not going to walk into the same place on the same night, right?"

Heather scowls at her. "It's Vegas, Mom. Of course they can."

Candi looks at me. "This man you saw, where did he go?"

"Down that hallway," I tell her, pointing back at it. "Which is more like a tunnel that leads into a cave." Then I throw in, "And it's roped off."

"We got kicked out," Heather tells her. "Gorilla Man's waiting around the corner."

I look at her. "Gorilla Man?" and I can't help it, I bust up.

But Candi's not listening. She marches her reheeled feet across the restaurant and disappears down the hallway. And as I'm watching her go, I get this icky feeling in my stomach that something's not right. And what's flashing through my mind while my stomach's churning is Heather's picture of her dad.

It looked just like Warren to me. It was a good, clear picture. If someone had seen him and then been shown that picture, they'd say, Yeah, I've seen that guy—even if his hair was shaggier.

But in all the places Heather had shown that picture around, she'd gotten nothing.

Zero hits.

It was my *mom* that people had identified.

Suddenly I'm wishing I could go back in time and show Heather's picture of her dad to the people who'd ID'd my mom. Because what if the fringed leather jacket and the Louis Vuitton sunglasses *weren't* just a change in style?

What if the guy in the fringed leather jacket *hadn't* been the Hollywood version of Warren Acosta?

What if it wasn't Warren at all?

But . . . why would my mom come to Las Vegas with Warren and spend the whole day with some other guy?

"What *are* you thinking?" Heather asks, her eyes squinting down on me.

"I'm thinking you should try calling your dad."

"What?"

"Try calling your dad."

"His phone's been off all day!"

"Please. Just try. Or text him. Something!"

"*Why?*"

"Well, you'd feel like an idiot, wouldn't you, if all this time you've been trailing someone who isn't your dad?"

"What?"

"Please. What's it going to hurt?"

While she's dialing, there's a commotion over by the tunnel hallway, and when I look, sure enough, Candi's getting ousted by Gorilla Man.

It's not a catch-air toss, but still.

Embarrassing.

And then Heather's saying, "Dad?" and I can tell by the size of her eyes she's reached more than his voice mail. "Where *are* you? . . . Are you serious? Well, we're here, too. . . . Yes, in Vegas! We've been chasing all over looking for you! . . . Mom and me!" She eyes me. "And Sammy . . . Yes, *that* Sammy . . . No!"

Candi's over with us now, and her eyes are huge. "Where is he?!"

Heather tells her, "He's at the airport!" But when Candi tries to get the phone, Heather shakes her off and plugs her ear.

"Is my mom with him?" I ask, but Heather doesn't answer me. Instead, she asks her dad, "What do you mean, you can't talk about it? You run off to Las Vegas to get married without . . . You didn't? Then why are you here?" There's a long pause and then she says, "Fine. She's right here," and hands Candi the phone.

Before Candi can take it, though, I reach out and practically beg, "Can I ask him one question? I promise I'll be quick."

Candi's dying for the phone herself, but she lets me have it, and I do my best to keep my promise. "Warren, it's Sammy. Is my mother with you?"

I can hear him take a deep breath, and when he finally lets it out, he says, "No."

"Is she okay?"

"She's fine."

"Is she still in Las Vegas?"

There's a big hesitation, and finally, "Yes."

"Where? And who's the guy in the fringed leather jacket?"

All I get is silence.

"Please! Tell me!"

"Look, Sammy, I can't."

"Why?"

"I just can't!"

My face flushes hot. "Okay, then just tell me this—is she going to a concert with him tonight at the House of Blues?"

A chuckle comes over the phone, and then he says, "Go get her, tiger."

The second Candi gets the phone, she wanders away from us with one finger in her open ear. "I think your mom dumped him," Heather says, but she doesn't sound mean or angry. She sounds worried.

"I tell you, she's a piece of work." I shake my head. "But we wanted them to break up, right?"

She frowns. "Right."

I kind of eye her and say, "Did he sound bad?"

"Yeah. Kind of." She shakes her head a little. "Maybe shocked?"

We're both quiet a minute, and then I say, "What I said to your mom before? It had to do with you and your dad, and her needing to tell him she still loves him. I didn't say anything about any of the . . . you know . . . other stuff."

She blinks at me.

That's all.

Just blinks.

I laugh. "I've never known you to be speechless before."

She blinks a few more times, then says, "And I've never known you to be *nice* before."

I laugh again. "Yeah, well, it's hard to be nice when you're constantly worried about being sabotaged."

Candi runs up, breathless and flushed. "I need you girls to get in a cab and go straight back to the hotel room."

"Why?" Heather asks. "Where are you going?"

"To the airport. To get your father."

"Wait!" Heather cries. "Why can't I just come with you?" She gives me a quick look. "Why can't *we* just come with you?"

"Because there are some things I need to say to your father, and I want to be alone." She hands back Heather's phone and gives her some cash, then tells her, "Give me your room key."

"My room key? Why?"

Candi puts out her hand. "Just give it to me."

So Heather does.

And Candi turns it over to me.

I look at her like, Huh? And she says, "Now I have a guarantee that you two will stick together." She looks at me. "And if Heather does ditch you, you just go let yourself into our hotel room. All our luggage is still there, and there's no way we're driving home tonight, so I'll see you both there." She turns to Heather. "Be nice, stick together, and leave your phone on." Then she kisses her on the cheek and says, "Wish me luck," and hurries off.

"Wow," I gasp as we watch her go.

"You mean holy smokes, right?"

I laugh. "Yeah, that's what I mean." Then I ask, "Can I borrow your phone?"

She hands it over. "Why *don't* you have one, anyway?"

Now, the way she asked wasn't mean—it was more like she was just curious. So I shake my head as I punch in my mother's number and say, "That's a good question."

"So what's the answer?"

"In a word? Finances."

"But . . . I thought you were rich!"

I laugh. "I'm not Marissa."

"But cell phones aren't *that* much. . . . Are you serious?"

I nod. "Life has not exactly been peachy." And since my mom's phone is still "unavailable," I end the call and hand the phone back. "I can give you the room key and you can go back to the MGM, but I need to stay here."

"Why?"

"I'm going to infiltrate the House of Blues."

"What?"

"You know—sneak into the concert?"

"How? Why? And Mom said we have to stick together!"

"How, I'm not sure. But my mom's in there, and since your dad won't tell me what happened or who the guy in the fringed jacket is, I'm going to find out for myself." I eye her. "So if you want to stick together . . ."

"You're asking me to go with you?"

I give a little shrug. "You're really sneaky. Could come in handy."

She smiles, and there's actually a *twinkle* in her eye. "Let's do it!"

And I can't help smiling back, 'cause something about the two of us feels unstoppable.

TWENTY

Obviously we had no chance of getting past Gorilla Man—especially since the line for the concert was now snaking into the casino, and big guys in red SECURITY T-shirts were standing by.

But Eddie-Elvis had said something about a Blues loading dock, which I figured meant the House of Blues loading dock.

Which I figured meant that there had to be a back way in.

"What are we looking for?" Heather asks after we've trucked through the casino for a minute.

"An exit."

"Not the main exit?"

"Well, the Elvises didn't cut across to the main exit. They kind of went this way, right?"

"But they could have turned anywhere in through here."

I nod. "I know. I just got the feeling they were going out this way."

"Maybe we don't have to go out to get in."

"What do you mean?"

"We could try going through there," Heather says, pointing to an EMPLOYEES ONLY door.

I grin at her. "You have no idea how funny that is." Then real quick I add, "I don't mean making-fun-of-you funny."

"Then what?"

"It's just that's something I would have said to Marissa."

"So? You want to try it? Maybe it goes backstage or something?"

We were already past the House of Blues, so I didn't think the door was connected, but I also didn't really understand how things were laid out. "So there's the House of Blues restaurant, and there's the gift shop, but where's the concert hall? Is it underground? I mean, that tunnel hallway thing slanted down, right?"

Heather nods. "And it went back behind the restaurant."

"So is that where all those people lined up are going? Down that hallway?"

"Must be."

I try to visualize where we'd walked and how the tunnel hallway had turned. "So the concert hall is, like, *that* way," I say, pointing.

She laughs, 'cause it turns out I'm pointing right at the EMPLOYEES ONLY door. And then, like it's egging us on, the door opens.

But only halfway.

And then it just stays like that.

Magically open.

Heather and I look at each other like, Whoa! And although there's a definite creep factor to this—like the witch inviting Hansel and Gretel inside her sugar-crusted house of horrors—we hurry over and get there in time to hear a woman's voice go, "No, here, I'll show you where it is," before the door starts to close.

We don't actually *see* anyone, and since there's a security keypad on the wall next to the door and the door has an automatic closer, there's no way we're going to get inside unless we move fast.

So I do what I always do when I don't want someone closing the door on me.

I stick my foot in.

"I hate when you do that," Heather whispers, 'cause let's just say I've gotten her in some major hot water by not letting a door or two shut when she would have liked them to.

I toss an innocent look at her. "You want me to let it close?"

"No, stupid."

I arch an eyebrow at her. "My name's Sammy."

"Sorry," she grumbles, and looks away.

So yeah. This was weird. And it wasn't just that I wanted to give whoever was on the other side of the door a chance to get gone. My foot stayed put because all of me was in a little bit of shock.

Heather saying she's sorry?

Like she means it?

Definitely weird.

Finally I pull the door open and stick my head inside, and what do I see?

A long, industrial-looking hallway with big steel

elevator doors on one side and regular metal doors on the other.

Heather wedges her head in, looks around, then pushes me through. "You can't be half in and half out—it looks suspicious!"

Which it does, only I've noticed something Heather hasn't.

Video cameras.

"Uh, I think we're already busted," I whisper as she heads for the elevators.

"What are you talking about?"

I hurry over to her and whisper, "Don't look, okay? But there are video cameras everywhere."

To my amazement, the only place she looks is straight at me. "Where?"

"In the ceiling corners. They got a straight-on shot of us sneaking through the door, and we're on camera right now."

"Great," she mutters, but instead of hightailing it back out of there, she presses the only button next to the elevator.

A button with an up arrow.

"Wait a minute," I tell her. "If this only goes up and we want to go *down* . . ."

"We want to go anywhere but here!" she whispers. "Away from the cameras!"

"But if it's not taking us where we *do* want to go . . . ?"

"We'll figure it out later!"

Then the elevator doors open and we find ourselves standing face to face with a security guard.

This guy is nothing like Gorilla Man. For one thing, he's wearing a blue uniform with official security-guy patches. For another, he's young and soft and has obviously never tossed anyone hard enough for them to catch air.

Still, from the look in his eye, I know we've hit the end of the line. So I pop off with "Hey, maybe *you* can help us!"

He steps out of the elevator but stays in front of it like he's going to stop us from making a dash inside. "Help you?" he says, giving me a doughy look. "I can sure help you *out* of here."

"Well, I don't know where we want to be, actually, in or out. My mom told me to meet her at the loading dock for the House of Blues."

"And what makes you think the loading dock is back here?"

"Well . . . I wouldn't think you'd have your *customers* loading and unloading stuff, right? *Employees* would do that. So it makes sense to go to where the employees are?" I give a little shrug. "At least, that's what we were thinking."

Heather nods and says, "And you're wearing blues— that's what they call them, right? Your uniform? So . . . we must be on the right track?"

He gives her a little squint. "My blues have nothing to do with the House of Blues blues. That's music. You know, wah-wah-wah, I got me a breaking heart?"

"Sounds like country music," I tell him. "Is it a country music place?"

"No! It's a *blues* place." He studies me. "You seriously don't know what the blues are?"

I give another little shrug, and Heather pipes up with "Personally, I'm just glad we ran into you so you can tell us where to go, because we are so lost, and this whole situation is ridiculous."

I scratch the back of my neck. "You can say that again."

Heather deadpans, "Personally, I'm just glad we ran into—"

"All right, all right!" Blues Boy says, then leads us back to the door we'd come through, saying, "Go out to the tram station—"

"There's a tram?"

He scowls at us. "Do you two always talk this much?"

Heather hitches a thumb my way. "*She* does. Good luck shutting her up. It's, like, constant."

I blink at her. "Look at you right now, yammering away! Besides, I only talk too much when I'm nervous. Or lost in Las Vegas. Or in some back hallway getting cuffed by a cop for trying to find my mother." I turn to Blues. "So okay, you're not cuffing me. At least I *hope* you're not going to. But—"

Mr. Security's just *staring* at me, so I pinch my lips and wait until finally he says, "Yes. There's a tram. It'll take you to the Luxor and the Excalibur. But you don't want to go to the Luxor or the Excalibur, so you don't want to get on the tram."

Now he's talking to us like we're stupid little kids, but that's all right. These stupid little kids are tricking their way out of getting detained or arrested or whatever *and* finding out how to get to the loading dock, all at the same time.

Heather eyes me and I eye her back, and we both just

let him keep talking down to us. "You want to go *past* the tram. Then keep walking *around* the building. The first down ramp you get to is the loading dock. Can't miss it."

I let go of my lip. "Do we go left past the tram or right?"

"Left."

"And the loading dock is also on the left?" Heather asks him.

He opens the door and gives us a condescending smile. "Very good."

"Well, thanks," we tell him, and the minute the door closes behind us, Heather gives a little snort and slyly puts out a fist for me to bump.

So I do.

It's just a little knock, but still.

Heather and I have bumped fists.

"So let's find the tram," she says, and I can tell she's feeling a little weird about it, too.

"Yeah, let's."

So we wander through the casino looking for signs that say TRAM, and pretty soon Heather spots one. "There!" she cries, pointing straight ahead.

So out we go to the tram depot, which is like a train depot only more high-tech and full of people wearing way too much gold lamé and perfume.

"Shoot me if I ever look like that," Heather whispers about a woman in a pink jumpsuit with oversized rhinestone jewelry.

"I've got your permission?" I whisper back. "'Cause you know, it seems wrong to first save someone's life and then shoot them."

She groans. "Don't remind me!"

Now, Casey had told me that my pulling Heather up from the bottom of a swimming pool last summer had made her hate me even harder, but it was something I'd never really understood. I mean, would she rather I'd let her drown? Hudson had explained that it was because she didn't want to owe me her life, especially since she obviously would like to kill me. Still—I'd never really been able to wrap my head around it.

So as we're heading down some steps and away from the tram holding area, I tell her, "I actually thought it was Marissa at the bottom of the pool."

Her head snaps to face me. "You *did*?"

The steps take us down to a walkway that goes through some landscaping between the building and a service road. So I follow that to the left, saying, "You were wearing the same swimsuit, remember?"

"Oh my God!" she cries, throwing her hands in the air. "All this time I thought you were trying to show off how you're a better person than me."

"By pulling you off the bottom of a pool?"

"Yeah! You could have sent anyone down after me! But no—you went and did it yourself." She grabs my arm and actually pogos up and down. "But you thought I was Marissa! You thought I was Marissa!"

"Which means . . . ?"

"Which means I don't owe you my life!"

I blink at her. "Wow. Hudson was right."

She stops jumping for joy. "That old guy? With the pink car?"

"Well, Hudson would insist the color's 'sienna rose,' but yeah. He said you hated owing me your life."

"But it turns out I *don't* owe you my life!" she says, letting go of my arm.

"I never thought you did."

"But *I* did!"

I shrug. "Well, even if you did, it's not like I'd make you be my house elf or something."

She eyes me. "I'd make a terrible house elf."

"Don't I know!" I laugh. "So forget it happened, would you?"

We keep on walking, with the backside of the Mandalay building on our left and the service road to our right. There are streetlights that help us see where we're going, and even though it's pretty isolated, it doesn't feel like we're in danger.

Well, unless we count each other as danger, which if we were back in Santa Martina, would have been a real thing.

Anyway, we finally come to a large opening in the building. It's like a giant cement garage, only without a roll-up door.

"Do you think that's it?" Heather asks, and even though we're still a ways away, she's whispering.

I give her a nod, then cut off the walkway and through some bushes to get us out of the streetlights. We head toward the edge of the building, and when we peek around the corner, what we see are two cars and a large panel truck parked at the end of a big cement delivery bay that's lit up by floodlights.

"Do you hear that?" I whisper, 'cause there's a steady thumping of music, fighting to be heard.

"This must be it!" She gets a little giddy and says, "I can't believe we're sneaking in to see Darren Cole!"

"I'm not sneaking in to see Darren Cole. I'm sneaking in to see my mom. And find out who she's with!"

"What's it matter anymore? As long as it's not my dad, right?"

I think about this a minute and grumble, "What kind of ditz comes to Las Vegas with one man and winds up with another?"

"Uh, your mother?" Heather laughs.

"Not funny."

She studies me a minute. "You're right. But what does it matter?"

"There's a lot you don't know, so just trust me—it matters. And the goal here is to help me find her, okay?"

"Fine, but if we actually *do* get inside and you actually *do* find her, I'm going to watch the concert while you deal with your mother."

"Okay . . . but then where do we meet afterward?"

She shrugs. "Back at the hotel room?"

"Then your mom will know we split up." I think. "How about back at the box office?"

"That works." She eyes my backpack and skateboard. "I know this is gonna be like ripping out your heart, but you have to leave your skateboard here. And nobody wears a backpack to a concert."

As much as I don't want to admit it, I know she's right.

So I take the rest of my reward money out of my backpack and stuff it in a front pocket of my jeans. And at the last minute I take my mother's picture, fold it, and put it in a back pocket. Then I stash the pack and my skateboard behind a hedge.

"Okay," Heather says. "Now, how are we going to pull this off?"

My heart's already starting to pound as I head out of the bushes and into the loading dock. "I have no idea."

TWENTY-ONE

There's a side door on the way down to the loading dock and a roll-up door at the end of it.

Both are locked.

So I head over to the panel truck.

"Wait!" Heather croaks out. "Where are you going?"

"To see how long that truck's been here."

"How are you going to tell that? And what's it matter?"

"If the hood's hot, it may have just gotten here. If it's cold, that means it's been a while and there's probably no one coming back out here."

"Why don't we just knock?"

"On the *door*?"

"Yeah! We'll make up some story, or—"

"They'll think we're groupies!"

"Of Darren *Cole*? He's way too old for us!"

"Groupies don't care!" I touch the hood of the truck, then head over to the cars to check them. "Or maybe the guitar player's young and cute or something."

"*He's* the guitar player."

"Okay, fine. The keyboard player, then."

"Nobody knows who the keyboard player is!"

"Well, maybe *you* don't, but a real groupie might."

"No. Nobody *ever* knows who the keyboard player is."

"They're cold," I say, changing the subject.

"For not knowing who the keyboard player is?"

"No! The hoods are all cold."

"Oh. I thought you were talking about groupies."

"I don't want to talk about groupies anymore, okay?" I look around, feeling like we've hit a total dead end. I mean, we *could* knock on one of the doors, and I *could* try showing the pictures of my mother to whoever answered, but how in the world would anyone be able to pick her out of a huge crowd of people coming in to see the concert?

And that's when something finally hits me.

And makes me feel like a complete moron.

My mother hadn't been in the crowd outside the House of Blues waiting for the concert to start. It had never even crossed my mind to look for her in the line, because I was sure she was already *inside*.

But why was she allowed inside if everyone else was blocked off or kicked out?

And the guy in the fringed jacket had walked in like he owned the place, so maybe he did.

Or had something to do with managing it.

Or maybe he managed the *band*.

Or was the publicist or an agent or a label guy . . . or whatever band people had in their, you know, entourage.

Or wait. Maybe he was *in* the band.

Maybe he was the keyboard player!

Vaguely I hear, "*What* is going on in your head?" and when I snap out of it, there's Heather, studying me like she's looking through a microscope.

So I tell her, "Your dad said—no, he *implied*—that my mom was going to see the Darren Cole concert tonight. And Elvis said he saw her go inside the House of Blues with the Fringed-Jacket Guy, and since the Fringed-Jacket Guy went right by the velvet rope without getting tossed on his ear—"

"Or rear."

"—that means my mother must have already been somewhere inside the concert hall."

"*That's* what you've been thinking? We knew that already!"

"But what that *means* is that the guy in the fringed jacket either works at the House of Blues or—"

"Is in the band!" She gasps and then covers her mouth. "Oh my God! Your *mother's* a groupie!"

"My mother's a . . . ? No! My mother's the *opposite* of a groupie. She is uptight and hates noise and blood and mice and has to be, you know, *perfect*."

"Who says groupies *like* noise and blood and mice?"

"You know what I mean! The point is, I *could* see her with some big-shot manager or agent or producer or something. Maybe it's some Hollywood hotshot who wants to put her in a movie. Or a video! He probably got them VIP seating and got let in early."

She looks at me like I've got beans for brains. "So she takes a trip to Las Vegas with my dad, happens to meet up with some bigwig producer, and dumps my dad on *Valentine's Day* to get a part in a movie?"

It does sound ridiculous, but the sad thing is, I could see my mother doing just that. "Why else would all this happen? She really liked your dad—she's not going to dump him to be some *groupie*."

Just then headlights turn into the loading bay and start coming toward us. Without a word, we both dive for cover behind the truck and hold our breath while the headlights get closer and closer . . . and then go off.

We hear a door slam and then the sound of another door sliding open, and when we finally peek out, we see a man in a turquoise shirt walking away from a van that says CONNIE'S CATERING in fancy turquoise lettering. He's carrying two big deli trays and heading straight for the back door of the House of Blues.

"It looks like he's working alone," Heather whispers.

"And I think he left the van's slider open," I whisper back, because I hadn't heard it close.

"Which means he's making more than one trip?"

I nod. "That's what I'm thinking."

We watch as he beats on the regular door, and when no one answers, he goes to the roll-up door and beats on that. It makes a lot more noise than banging on the regular door did, and after he does it twice, someone inside rolls the door up.

The music goes from thumping to *loud,* and the combination of an open door and a rock concert must have overloaded Heather's logic circuits, because she starts to make a break for it.

I yank her back. "No! You'll get busted!"

"So what are we going to do? Sit here and watch the door close?"

It turns out that's exactly what we do. Only before it closes, a big guy in a red SECURITY T-shirt steps out from inside and looks all around like he's making sure nobody's out in the loading dock planning to infiltrate the House of Blues.

"So now what?" Heather says after the door's rolled down.

I tap her arm as I move out. "Come on."

"*Now?*"

"Shh! Just follow me."

So I lead her around to the van's open door, and what do we see inside?

A whole bunch of deli trays and bakery boxes and baskets of fruit.

I also see some turquoise polo shirts on hangers, dangling from a hook on the side of the van.

"We're wide-open here!" Heather whispers. "What are we *doing*?"

So I grab two of the shirts and we zip back around to the far side of the van. "Here," I tell her. "Put this on over your clothes."

She doesn't say, That'll look dorky! or anything like it. She just puts it on.

And yeah, she looks dorky.

But then, so do I.

Anyway, I peek up through the van's side window, where we've got a clear view of the building. And we don't have to wait long before the regular door starts to open.

Heather grabs my arm. "There he is!" And as we're watching him stoop over to wedge some paperwork down by the threshold so the door won't latch, she suddenly looks at me and says, "Is this what it's like to be Marissa?"

"Huh?"

She shakes her head a little. "Never mind."

But it does sink in, so I tell her, "Actually, yes. I'm always dragging her into *something*." I eye her. "Not so much dragging going on with you. I'm more having to hold you back."

"Yeah, well, you were right—this is definitely a better plan."

If we had been doing something less, you know, adrenaline-intensive, I would probably have fainted. But seeing how we were about to dive into some security-infested waters, I didn't actually pass out from shock. I just let her words kind of ring in my ears.

Anyway, the catering guy is heading back for another load now, so we duck down, and when we're sure he's walking off with the second load, Heather whispers, "We're grabbing a tray, right? And going in?"

"That's the plan. We've just got to time it right."

"We want him to be in long enough to be far enough away—like in the greenroom, right? But not so long that he's on his way out when we're coming in with his trays?"

"Bingo."

The catering guy goes back through the regular door,

and even though it looks like it closes, I can tell the door's not latched.

"So . . . when?" Heather whispers.

"Not yet."

Ten seconds go by.

"Now?"

"Not yet."

"Now?"

"No."

"So . . . when?"

"Going by his last trip, I'd say"—I give her a grin—"*now.*"

So we zip around the van, grab a deli tray each, and beeline for the door the catering guy went through. Sure enough, it's not latched.

Since the roll-up door is to the right, I whisper, "Once we're in, I'm planning to go to the left and walk like I know where I'm going."

She nods. "Let's do it."

Opening the door and stepping in is like entering a dark cave with a searchlight behind us. I can see a tall slice of light to our left, but where we are is dark except for the light coming in from outside.

"Quick, close it!" I tell Heather.

She does, and as we hurry to the left like we'd planned, she nods at the tall slice of light. "That's the stage!" she calls over the music.

And yeah, there's no doubt about it—we are backstage at a rock show.

There's also no doubt that we've been spotted by security. "Gorilla at two o'clock," I tell Heather.

"Two o'clock?" But then she sees him. And where he'd just been watching us before, now he's coming at us.

"What do we do?" Heather says in my ear, and I can tell she is freaking out.

"We stay cool!" I tell her back, and instead of trying to ditch it through the dark somewhere, I move *toward* him.

"Third door down!" he shouts over the music.

"Thanks!" I shout back, and even though my heart is beating louder than the drums onstage, I head off in the direction he's pointing like everything's cool.

When we're in the clear, I sneak a grin at Heather, and she sneaks one back.

We have infiltrated the House of Blues!

TWENTY-TWO

There was no way I was going down to the third door.

That's where the real caterer had to be!

And since the first door we came to was propped open, I ducked inside without looking back.

Which turned out to be a classic case of jumping out of the frying pan and into the fire. There were three scruffy-looking guys hanging around on couches. Maybe none of them were Gorillas in red shirts, but they had a really, uh . . . *hungry* look to them. Like they were amped and armed and ready to slay dragons.

Or in this case, girls with food trays.

"Dude, you're serious?" one of the guys says, instantly moving from sitting on the couch to standing on it.

The guy next to him eyes us, but instead of jumping up, he slouches farther into the cushions. "They got the wrong room," he grumbles. "Darren Cole's having an after-party."

The first guy springs off the couch and hurries over to close the door. And while he's doing that, the third one perks up like he's caught the scent of warm blood. And then the first guy checks out my tray and cries, "Dude, it's *sushi*."

"Hang on!" I snap. "You're not getting this for nothing."

"Oh, really?" the first guy says, and he obviously thinks I'm hilarious.

"Oh, you can *steal* it from us," I tell him, "but then we'll sic the Gorilla Gang on you, and good luck with them!"

"The Gorilla Gang?" the third guy says.

"Security, doofus," the Sloucher calls over.

The first guy stares at me like he can't quite believe I've got the guts to go up against three scruffy guys with tattoos. So I tell him, "Look, all we want are badges."

"Badges?"

I point at the laminated backstage pass hanging from a cord around his neck. "Two of those," I tell him, "for two trays of sushi."

"Dude!" The main guy laughs as he looks at the other two. "They're groupies!"

The Sloucher calls, "Not for Hallowgram."

"Who's Hallowgram?" Heather asks.

"The guys out there rocking the house down?" the main guy snaps. "The opening act?"

"Oh," Heather says, not sounding at all impressed.

"See?" the Sloucher calls. "We get squat." He eyes the main guy. "And I know you're a big fanboy, but I'm getting pretty tired of hauling their gear for beer."

"So let's have sushi!" The main guy whips off his badge and looks at the others. "Who's giving up their badge to share this feast with me?"

Suddenly badges are flying at us and our food trays are being taken and the main guy is giving me a crooked smile, saying, "Our little secret."

So while they turn their backs on us and descend on the food, Heather and I whip off our turquoise shirts, stuff them under a couch, loop backstage passes over our heads, and hurry out of there.

"This is *awesome!*" Heather squeals.

"Stay cool," I tell her as I lead her farther away from the outside door we'd come through.

"Do you think we can get into Darren Cole's after-party?"

"Staaaay cooool. First we have to find a place to disappear for a while."

"Disappear? Why? We have backstage passes! We can go anywhere!"

Right then the catering guy steps out of Door Number Three. Luckily, we can see him a lot better than he can see us because of the light coming out of the room he was in. So I grab Heather and move deeper into the darkness of the big backstage curtain while he hurries by.

Heather's neck cranes around as she watches him go. "Do you think he'll notice the trays are missing?"

"Stop looking!" I tell her. "We just need to disappear!"

When we get to the end of the backstage curtain, there's another clear view of the stage, and since there's nobody standing in the wings, I move in a few steps to see if I can figure out where my mother might be. There are huge speakers and other equipment between us and the band, so it's actually really easy to sneak a little ways onto the stage and still be totally hidden. Trouble is, the stage lights are really bright, which makes looking past the stage hard to do. What I *can* see is that there's a big standing area in front of the stage and a whole raised level of seating that curves up and back to a big open balcony. Like a theater where the bottom got dropped down to make room for a giant dance floor and a stage.

And really, all this tells me is that the place is huge.

Then Heather's in my ear saying, "If the guy in the fringed jacket has anything to do with Darren Cole or his band, they'll be in the greenroom."

"What greenroom?"

"You know—Door Number Three? Where all the food was getting delivered? They're probably hanging out there right now, waiting for these guys to be done playing." She nods past the stage. "You'll never find her if she's out there. And why would she be out there if she got in early?"

Which all made sense.

But still.

Something about going into Darren Cole's greenroom scared me.

"Sammy! Come on! Do you want to find her or not?"

"I can't just walk in and say I'm looking for my mother! So what do I say? What's our story?"

"Why can't we just walk in and look around?"

"We're thirteen! Someone will ask what we're doing there! And if we blow it and get busted, there goes my chance of finding her."

"You worry too much. Come on. We'll just wing it."

"No!"

She grabs me by the sleeve. "Come on!"

The next thing I know, Heather's yanking me through Door Number Three, and there we are, two thirteen-year-olds, in the middle of at least a dozen over-thirty-year-olds. There's a guy noodling on a guitar, another guy lacing up his black running shoes, another guy tapping drumsticks on the arm of a couch, and a whole bunch of women doing a whole lot of nothing besides showing skin.

"She's not here," I whisper to Heather. "And I don't see a fringed jacket anywhere."

"So let's ask."

"No! Let's get *out* of here!"

"Why are you so weirded out?" she asks me when we're safely outside.

"I don't know, okay? I'm . . . I'm . . ." But everything's a jumble and I just can't put it into words.

"You're what? A few minutes ago, you were playing hardball for backstage passes. And now you're totally wimped out! What happened?"

"I've . . . I've got this really weird feeling. Like a panic attack, only . . . only I don't know why!"

She studies me a minute. "Maybe you don't really want to find her."

Something about that felt close. And then out of my mouth comes "Or maybe I just don't want to know who she's with." I shake my head. "I need to sit down."

"Sit down!? You don't sit down at a rock concert!"

And really, I couldn't explain why I felt so weak and

pukey and confused all of a sudden. It was like this *force* had come over me and broken up all the steely bonds that had been holding my anger molecules together.

My mom had secrets from me, but maybe she had secrets for a reason.

Maybe I really was better off not knowing.

So I tell Heather, "Go and do whatever you want. I need to find a place to sit down. I'll meet you out at the box office after the show."

She grumbles something I can't understand, then grabs me by the arm and yanks me along until we're way past the stage and she sees a set of stairs on our left, going up. "Here," she says, sort of pushing me down on a stair tread. "Sit."

And then she sits next to me.

"Maybe it's just too loud?" she asks, checking me over.

I shake my head, because it *is* loud, but not loud enough to make me freak out like this. "Something's wrong," I finally say.

"With you? With your mom?"

"With this whole situation!"

"Look. I'm going to go back into Door Number Three and ask if anyone knows Lana Keyes. Or the guy with the fringed jacket. And if they throw me out . . . well, you can go search for her yourself and I'll meet you at the box office."

I blink at her.

And blink some more.

Then we hear the band onstage announce, "We've got one more for you!" And since I know I'm running out of time, I make myself stand up and say, "I'll do it. You get down there and watch Darren Cole."

"Really?"

"No sense in both of us getting kicked out."

She watches me head back to Door Number Three, so when I reach it, I wave her off, then go inside.

"Excuse me!" I call, holding up the picture card of my mother. "Has anybody seen this woman?" I sort of parade it around, and since nobody's jumping up going, Yeah! I know her! I add, "Or a guy in a fringed leather jacket?"

The minute I say that, there's a shift—a sudden stillness that tells me something's changed.

Like shifting plates way beneath the ocean.

"Who wants to know?" the guy with the drumsticks asks, and I can tell—the waters are rising and I'm about to be slammed to shore.

So as casually as I can, I start to backpedal.

Or really, back*paddle*.

And while people in the room start whispering to the person next to them, I do the only thing I can think to do.

Dive for the door!

TWENTY-THREE

I make a break for the stairs, and in my hurry to get gone, I plow right into Heather.

"What happened?" she asks as I stumble around her.

"What are you still doing here?"

"What do you think, stupid?"

I let it slide and charge for the stairs. I had no idea where they led, but up seemed way better than anywhere behind the stage. "Something weird is going on."

"What do you mean?" she asks, chasing after me.

"The whole room went quiet when I asked about the guy in the fringed jacket."

"So?"

"So when it goes from *you* asking questions to *them* asking questions, it's time to leave."

"Why? Why not just answer the questions?"

I can't exactly tell her that my not answering questions comes from years of conditioning. Or that living somewhere illegally makes you jumpy. Especially around adults asking questions. So I just race ahead and tell her, "Because the vibe in the room went bad."

"The vibe," she says, like it's the most ridiculous thing she's ever heard.

"Yes!" We're at the top of the stairs now, and since the only open avenue is a U-turn down a hallway, I zip around the handrail and keep moving. The music has switched from live and loud to canned and pretty quiet, so I can hear someone pounding up the stairs, shouting, "I think she went up here!"

I try a door labeled JAMES BROWN, but it's locked. "Bail out anytime," I tell Heather as I charge ahead. "I'm busted."

But in this hallway there are no other doors, and there sure doesn't seem to be any way for her to bail out.

Especially since there's definitely someone with a flashlight coming up behind us.

So we just charge forward until we come to a quick little zigzag in the hallway, and once we're through that, we find ourselves in a wide-open area with big square pillars and couches and a bar and people hanging around, laughing and drinking, checking out the outsider art that's all over the pillars and walls or looking over the balcony at the stage.

I search around for my mom or a fringy maroon jacket as I try to disappear between people. Everyone's wearing a VIP badge, but besides not having one of those, we're obviously not old enough to be hanging out in the House of Blues bar balcony. Plus, there aren't actually that many people—only a few dozen total—so vanishing in the crowd isn't exactly an option.

But running is!

Especially since I can see now that the guy following us is a Gorilla.

And he's got a walkie-talkie.

"Bail out!" I tell Heather. "He's after me, not you."

She stays right behind me. "He knows I'm with you!"

"He can't be two places at once, right? If you get the chance, bail!"

But she stays with me as I jet across the balcony and find myself *again* being only able to go down a dark hallway.

Well, unless I want to stand around and wait for the elevator doors in front of me to open, but the Gorilla's coming, so who's got time for that?

So down the hallway I charge, looking for *anywhere* to disappear. But it's just like the other side—no doors at all! We've run in a giant U on the level above the stage, and I'm pretty sure if we don't find a place to hide, we'll wind up going down another set of stairs and be back near the loading dock door—back where we'd started!

But going in a giant U and disappearing somewhere downstairs is better than getting busted, so I keep charging ahead.

And then all of a sudden there's a light coming *toward* us.

So yeah. We're pinned between two beams of Gorilla light.

"Shoot!" I cry, but on our right there's a door that says ETTA JAMES.

In my little mental map, it seems like we're right across the stage from the James Brown door we'd tried earlier, so

I'm sure this one will be locked, too. And even if it's not, where could it possibly go? It's hopeless. I know it's hopeless. We're just flailing fish in a big Gorilla net.

Still, with one last desperate wiggle, I try the door.

And it opens.

Without a word, I grab Heather and whoosh us both inside, then turn around quick and lock the door. And when I turn back, what I see is Heather with her eyes popped and her jaw dropped. And since Heather never shows much more expression than a sneer, I know she must be seeing something really gnarly, so I actually *jump* to get away from the corner where she's staring.

The room we're in is small—about the size of a big walk-in closet—and dark except for light coming in through a sort of balcony opening, which looks like it leads to stage lights ahead and death below.

And I'm in such a state that what flashes through my mind is that whatever's in the corner must be vicious or deadly or horrendously ugly for Heather to be looking so scared. Like maybe a decaying corpse hung from the ceiling, or a rabid serpent with foamy fangs and beady black eyes about to strike, or a—

And then I turn and see the monster myself.

A monster with buggy eyes and glistening teeth.

A monster that speaks.

"*Samantha?* Samantha, what are you *doing* here?"

Apparently the Gorilla Force has a key to the Etta James room, because two guys in red shirts and the guy with the drumsticks from Darren Cole's greenroom all barge in.

"We okay?" the guy with the drumsticks asks my mom after he sizes things up.

My mother nods, but she's still just staring at me, stunned.

Drumsticks asks, "That's her?" and when my mom nods again, he points his sticks at Heather. "Her sister?"

"Oh, no," my mother gasps. "Her friend."

Normally, I would have corrected that, but at this point I'm too confused and shocked and just weirded out to even care. I mean, maybe I'd been tracking my mother all day, but actually *finding* her, and finding her in this oversized closet by herself?

It was so hard to wrap my head around.

And then I notice that this oversized closet has an open bottle of champagne and two glasses on a table by a couch.

Champagne?

My mother has some quick signaling exchange with Drumsticks, who tells the Gorillas, "It's all cool up here. Sorry for the false alarm."

One of the Gorillas says, "You want I should bring up skybox badges?"

Drumsticks looks at my mother. "They'll be with you, right?"

My mother looks at me, then Heather, then me. "Uh . . ."

"Uh?" I snap. "Really? After everything we've been through to find you, all you can say is uh?"

"What I *mean*, Samantha, is that I'd like to speak with you privately. I just didn't want to be rude to Heather."

"Oh!" Heather says. "Don't worry about me!" She turns to Drumsticks and the Gorillas and says, "Can you get me down in the pit?"

Drumsticks laughs. "The show doesn't get moshers."

"I don't care! I just want to be down there!"

He laughs again. "Well, *that* I can arrange. Follow me."

So they take off, and then it's just me and my mother. I watch as she collapses onto the couch and heaves a big, heavy sigh.

Very un-Lady-Lana-like.

And so is her posture. She's—gasp—*slouched.*

And her face is sagging.

Like she's just too tired to pretend to be perfect anymore.

Finally she shakes her head a little and says, "I will never understand your grandmother."

I almost blurt out, Grams? Why her? but it hits me that she thinks I know something I don't. So I just bite my tongue and wait.

She cocks her head. "Where is she, anyway? Didn't want to suffer through 'that racket,' am I right? So she sends two thirteen-year-old girls in alone? I can't believe she brought you here."

But instead of answering, I nod at the champagne glasses and turn it back on her with "Forget Grams. Where is *he*, huh?"

She takes a deep breath and closes her eyes. "None of this is his fault." Her eyes flutter open and she says, "I've made so many mistakes. *So* many mistakes."

I frown at her. "I think Warren would agree with that."

She studies me. "It's so strange to hear you call him Warren."

"Well, I sure wasn't going to call him Dad—not until I found out who my real dad was. But it looks like I won't have to worry about calling him that anyway." And even though the last thing I wanted was for her to marry Casey's dad, all of a sudden I'm mad. "Warren's a nice guy. How could you come here with him and just *dump* him? What is *wrong* with you? How can you just *discard* people?"

She gives me a pleading look. "I didn't mean for this to happen! It's been fourteen years since I've seen him! Fourteen and a half! I thought I was over him! I thought I was in love with Warren! I wanted to resolve things so I could move on! Warren offered to come along for moral support, and we were going to make a Valentine's weekend out of it, but . . . but then I saw him and it all came flooding back and Warren could tell and . . . and . . . oh, Samantha I've wasted so much time. So much life!"

I was used to my mom and her dramatic explanations. Her woe-is-me rationalizations for being a self-absorbed diva. But something in my brain hitched.

It was like a locomotive thought had backed into a train car thought—*c-clank*—then started pulling forward.

Fourteen years, she'd said. Fourteen and a half.

Why did the half even matter?

The locomotive starts gaining steam and makes me a little weak at the knees.

The half *did* matter.

I sort of stagger to a chair by the balcony wall, and

over the wall I can see the stage below me—the flaming-heart House of Blues backdrop, the dimmed stage lights, the drum kit and amps and monitors and microphones, all behind the closed stage curtain.

There'd been background music playing between bands, but now it's off and musicians are taking their positions onstage. I recognize Drumsticks and two other guys from the greenroom, and there are a couple of guys in black T-shirts zipping around connecting cables and delivering water bottles.

And when the T-shirt guys are done doing their thing, Drumsticks clicks his sticks and the band starts playing. And without anyone announcing the band or anything, the curtain goes up.

The music is *loud,* and it's shaking my chest, and the crowd is whooping and cheering and then goes wild when out onto the stage walks Darren Cole with a guitar strapped over what he'd been wearing all day.

A fringed maroon jacket.

TWENTY-FOUR

It took longer than it should have to sink in—maybe because it was so hard to believe. Still, everything about it made sense. From the fourteen and a half years to the way Grams got all uptight when I'd sing "Waiting for Rain to Fall" to the bizarre trip to Las Vegas to why my mother had refused to talk to me about who my dad was.

I turn away from the stage to face her, and over the music I shout, "You were a *groupie*?"

"No!" she shouts back. "How can you even *say* that!" I look at her like, Du-uh, so she shouts, "He was my boyfriend!"

"Did he know about me?"

"No!"

"Well, does he now?"

"Yes!"

And because I still can't believe it and just need to hear it from her, I shout, "So Darren Cole is my father."

"Yes!"

"All this time, Darren Cole has been my father."

"Yes!"

"So *why* couldn't you tell me this?"

"Because I hadn't told him!"

"And that was more important than answering me all those times I asked?"

"At first you were too young to understand! And then I . . . I didn't want you to think I was a floozy!"

"So instead you let me think that my dad was an ax murderer or maybe a child molester or the leader of a cult in the backwoods of Oregon!"

"I never gave you any reason to believe any of those things!" She squints at me. "And *Oregon*? Why would I ever go to Oregon?"

"Because you were in love with a cult leader!"

"But *Oregon*?"

"Of everything I've said, *that's* what you're fixating on? Oregon?"

She does some doe-eyed blinking but doesn't actually *say* anything.

"Look," I shout at her, "when something doesn't make sense, I try to *make* it make sense! People join cults! Trees grow! I can't help it! You made my dad a deep dark secret, so of course I thought there was something awful about him! But no—*you* were embarrassed. It was something *you* were ashamed of! I should have known because it's *always* about you!"

She holds her head and shouts, "We really cannot have this conversation now. Can we please wait until the concert's over? Then we can discuss the whole thing."

I just stare at her.

She wants me to wait for the concert to be over?

The concert is more important than talking to me?

Plus it's so stupidly *typical* of Lady Lana to want to put off talking about this that I just get up and shout, "You know what? I need to go get my skateboard before someone steals it."

"Your *skateboard*? Your skateboard is more important than seeing your dad perform?"

I stare at her. "Seeing that guy perform is more important than talking to me?"

"I *am* talking to you! But it's impossible with music at this volume!"

"And this is the only place we can talk?"

She doe-eyes me again.

"See ya!" I shout, and even though she says, "Samantha!" I go out the door, and of course she doesn't follow.

The farther away from the skybox I get, the madder I get. Here I'd spent the whole day trying to find my mother, and now all I want is to get away from her. And I really *do* want my skateboard. I'm dying to get on it and *escape*.

One of the Gorillas who'd cornered me in the skybox is stationed at the bottom of the stairs when I find my way down. "I need to go outside!" I yell over the music.

He gives me a single nod, then walks me over to the loading dock door that Heather and I had come through, keys in the unlock code, and lets me out. "You comin' back?" he calls as I storm off.

"No!" I shout, which I know is really, really stupid, but I'm so crazed from everything that I don't care if I'm locked out in the dark in Las Vegas.

Anything's better than being with my mother.

Now, part of my brain is trying to tell me to slow down

and quit being stupid, but the rest of me isn't listening. I march up to the bushes, look in the *wrong* bushes, start to lose it because I think my stuff's been stolen, see that it's buried in the next bush over, about break down over *that*, then strap on my pack, grab my board, get to the sidewalk, and take off.

And really, I don't know why I'm so upset. I mean, come on. My dad's not a serial killer. Or a crazy cult leader. Or a priest.

He's a rock star!

But . . . I didn't want a rock star dad.

Well, okay. It was better than having him be a serial killer or a crazy cult leader or a priest, but what I really wanted was someone . . . normal. A guy who could figure out how to be a good dad.

That is so *not* a rock star.

Rock stars make *rotten* dads. They don't have time for their kids, they have groupies galore, and they think they're all that with their guitars and their hair and their stupid fringed maroon jackets.

Who wants that?

Especially when you've already got a diva mom?

Normally, riding my skateboard helps me think. I get all my frustrations out by pawing at the sidewalk and jumping curbs, which frees my mind to sort things out, *think* things out, and come up with a plan. But this time I could barely even see where I was going because I was crying.

I'm talking crying with *hiccups*.

And I guess I was over the legal limit of emotions for operating a skateboard, because I wound up doing something I'd never done while flying along dry-eyed—I caught a wheel on the edge of the walkway and went catapulting into some plants.

Plants that had just been watered.

So yeah. I was an emotional mess, and now I was a muddy mess, too. And all of a sudden I was just *so* tired that I couldn't seem to do anything but sit there on wet plants and sob like someone had died.

Which was stupid.

Nobody had died!

Still, that's what it felt like. And I was too jumble-brained to figure out why, so I kept sitting there sobbing like a poor pathetic idiot.

What made me finally get up was water soaking through the seat of my jeans. "Great!" I moaned. But being wet on the bottom at least made me quit the waterworks on top.

Until I picked up my skateboard out of the little ditch it had landed in.

Right away I saw that one of the front wheels was crooked. *Loose.* "Great!" I moaned again, and had to really fight the tears. And I was so mad at myself! After all the miles my board had carried me, I ran it into a ditch and broke it?

I tried to figure out if I could fix it, but that was hopeless, too. And there's only so long you can stand around in the cold in the dark in a ditch looking at your poor broken skateboard before you decide to do something—anything—else.

So I started walking.

Not back the way I'd come.

Forward.

I didn't know where I was going or what I was going to do, but somehow it felt like there was no going back. So I just walked and walked, lugging my poor broken skateboard around the huge Mandalay Bay property, thinking about how much *worse* things were now than they'd been before. It wasn't just my skateboard—everything about my life felt broken. Instead of having more family, I felt like I had less. Grams and I were in a big fight, and after what I'd told Candi . . . well, there was no way I could fix that. And my mother was even more of a stranger than she'd been before, and my dad was someone who was definitely going to resent me, too.

I mean, what rock star wants to deal with some surprise kid?

Oh, by the way, Darren, she's yours.

Can you say paternity test?

Or *gold digger*?

Plus, now I was stuck in a horrible showdown about whose problem I was. My mother'd already pushed me onto Grams, so obviously she didn't want the responsibility. And it's not like she'd sat me down and told me who my dad was and let me decide what I wanted to do about contacting him. No, she'd gone to Darren Cole—a guy she hadn't seen in fourteen years—and dropped the bomb without even giving me a *hint*.

And she'd done it shortly after her stupid soap had been canceled!

Coincidence?

I don't think so!

So yeah. Instead of feeling like I had more family, I felt like I had *none*. Like I'd lost what was left of my mother, the potential of a father, and Grams, all in one day.

And my skateboard was toast!

So I walked and moped and just felt lost. And so *defeated*. When I saw an empty bench on a walkway leading over to the big pyramid, I thumped onto it and *sat* and moped.

I was clueless about what to do. I was cold and exhausted, and I sure didn't want to go back to the House of Blues, but the only other choice I had was going to Heather and Candi's room at the MGM. The scary thing is, I would *rather* have done that, but something about choosing Heather and Candi over my mother made me feel like I'd hit rock bottom.

Plus, I didn't feel like I could talk to Marissa about it. She would not get why it was the opposite of awesome. Not when her own dad was making the whole family miserable. My problems would look like a dream next to hers.

And Casey?

What was I going to say to him?

Uh, we need to get a new song.

I mean, we'd *kissed* to "Waiting for Rain to Fall."

Dis-turb-ing!

Besides, I'd stood him up on Valentine's Day.

What kind of rotten girlfriend was I?

Still, even thinking about talking to Casey gave me a glimmer of not being alone, so I looked at my watch, wondering if I should call.

"Eleven-thirty?!" I gasped.

Well, at least he'd be home. And since his mom and sister weren't, there was no problem calling him this late.

So yeah, I wound up going back to Mandalay Bay.

Back through the lobby.

Back through the casino.

Back past the House of Blues box office and the Darren Cole poster.

Back around the corner and, this time, clear through the mini food court to the pay phone.

I'd decided that I'd start with I'm sorry. But I couldn't seem to figure out what to say after that. So after standing around for five minutes worrying about it, I finally decide that I'm sorry is a good start and dial his home number.

It rings.

And rings.

And somewhere in the fuzz of my brain, it registers that my heart actually hurts.

And after two more rings, it turns into a deep, hard ache.

One that seems like it could actually kill me.

And when he doesn't answer, I just slide to the floor, and there they come again.

Tears.

And I'm just sitting there crying, feeling so completely alone, when I hear a voice shout, "She's right there!"

I look over, and there's Heather with a Gorilla.

The same Gorilla who'd let me out the back door.

He comes racing over like he's just found his long-lost puppy. "Are you hurt?"

I fling away the tears and grumble, "I'm fine."

He snatches a walkie-talkie off his belt and steps away

while Heather swoops in and says, "I can't believe you're out here crying! The guy in the fringed jacket was Darren Cole!"

"Yeah, I know."

"So? No wonder your mother dumped my dad!" Then she gets all flushed and excited and swoony as she says, "Instead of moping out here, you should have come down in the pit with me. The concert was *amazing*. And the bass player is so hot!"

I look right at her. "You're serious?" And suddenly I get that I'm going to have to deal with a whole new problem.

A *huge* one.

Heather Acosta thinks we should be friends.

Then I add, "The concert's over?" because really, I feel like I'm in some weird Möbius strip where I'm on one side of time and everyone else is on the other.

The Gorilla puts out a hand, and I let him pull me to my feet. "I need to take you back inside. I can't transmit from out here."

"I don't want to go back in there!"

"Please. I'm in deep sh—stuff for letting you out."

"Why?"

"I just am, okay?"

So I let him nudge me along, through the restaurant, down the ramp, past the velvet rope, and down the hallway tunnel into a wide area with small tables crammed against a railing that's a little bit above the dance floor. And while he's on his walkie-talkie saying stuff like "I've got her" and "Will do," Heather's whispering, "Do you think we'll get to go to the after-party?" and "Your mom'll want to introduce you to him, right?" making it so I can't really hear what the Gorilla on the other end is saying.

"I can't *believe* this!" Heather squeals. "This has been the best night of my *life*."

Drumsticks is coming toward us, and when he's close enough, Heather jets forward and says, "My name's Heather, by the way, and the show was *awesome*."

He nods and gives her a grin and says, "I'm Marko." Then he looks at me with one eyebrow cranked. "Lana was really worried."

I snort. "Yeah, right."

The eyebrow cranks up a little higher, but he doesn't say anything back. Instead, he tells the Gorilla, "Thanks, man. I'll take it from here," and leads us through a gate and onto the stage, where a small crew is coiling up cables and shuttling gear offstage. And while Heather's all excited about being *on the stage*, I'm feeling totally awkward. I mean, I don't know this Marko drummer dude, but obviously he knows Lady Lana.

And I guess he's feeling a little awkward, too, 'cause he finally says, "I've been with Darren since the beginning. This is some surprise."

"You can say that again," I grumble.

He eyes me. "You didn't know?"

"I tracked my mother down and figured it out myself. Tonight. In the skybox."

His eyebrows go flying. "Whoa." Then he grins and says, "Well, you must be pretty stoked."

"No!" I snap at him. "I am not pretty stoked! I'm pretty ticked off!"

"What is going on?" Heather says through her teeth as we pass by the backstage curtains.

I practically bite her head off with "Nothing, okay?" but obviously there's no avoiding the truth.

Especially since Drumsticks takes us into the greenroom.

And Darren Cole is standing right there.

TWENTY-FIVE

There are about a dozen people in the greenroom. All the Troublemakers, plus some women.

And the Diva.

The food trays are open and so are a bunch of bottles of champagne. And I guess everyone knew the situation, because the minute we walk through the door, the talking peters out until it's dead quiet.

"That's her?" Darren whispers to my mother.

Only he's looking right at Heather.

Now, Heather's dressed like . . . well, like she's been to the best stores at the mall.

Me, I'm dressed like I've been to the thrift store.

Because I have.

My jeans are worn and tattered to begin with, and now they're also muddy and still kinda wet. My high-tops are splitting out the sides, my T-shirt and sweatshirt are frayed around the edges, and I haven't brushed my hair since this morning—which suddenly feels like a hundred light-years ago.

So yeah. Obviously I'm from a different universe than Queen-of-Drama Lana.

Obviously Heather is much more what a surprise daughter should look like.

"Uh, no," Lady Lana says, and she's now beet red. "That's her friend." And I guess she's embarrassed by the way I look *and* the way I'm "glowering," because she starts making excuses for me, saying, "She's upset because her grandmother told her before I could."

"Grams did *not* tell me!" I snap. "Grams has nothing to do with me being here!"

"Then . . ." She looks from me to Heather.

"I didn't come with Heather, either! She came with Candi. They drove, I flew. But we're all here because we thought you'd come to Vegas to marry *Warren*."

"Who told you that!?"

Everyone in the room is dead quiet and *staring* at me, but I don't care. I give my mother a hard look. "When you don't answer questions . . . when you shut off your phone . . . when you have a history of *hiding* things, people jump to conclusions! And since I didn't want a second dad when I didn't even know who—"

"Samantha," my mother begs, "can we *please* do this later."

"No! You always want to talk about things later, and we never do! And I want you to know that to *get* here . . . to *get* here and finally get some answers, I stowed away in the McKenzes' car to get to the airport, because Marissa and her mom were taking an emergency trip here to bail her dad out of . . . out of a *jam*, and while they went through airport security, I bought my own ticket pretending I was with them, and when we landed in Vegas, I told

234

Mrs. McKenze that you were supposed to pick me up, and when you didn't show up, I went through this big, complicated chess game of moves so that I would have a place to sleep, but instead of sleeping, I went through the phone book looking up wedding chapels trying to find where you were registered and—"

"But I wasn't coming here to get married! I came here to talk to Darren! Warren came along for moral support!"

"So why would he buy expensive jewelry right before coming here?"

"Jewelry? What jewelry? And how did you hear that?"

"Yeah," Heather says to me. "How did *you* hear that?"

I zoom in on Heather and say through my teeth, "You want me to tell her your mom was having your dad investigated?" That shuts her up quick, so I turn back to my mom and say, "The point is, you never tell me anything! And since your phone was off, obviously you didn't want to be disturbed! So I called a friend of mine who's an Elvis impersonator here and—"

"You have a friend who's an Elvis impersonator?"

"It's something that happens when you get sent to the market at midnight because your blackmailing neighbor needs Tums."

"What?"

"Which of course you know nothing about because you're too busy being *you* to worry about *me* and my blackmailing neighbors."

"Blackmailing neighbors?" Heather asks.

"Never mind!" my mom and I say at the same time. Then I turn back to Lady Lana. "But it's a good thing I got sent out for Tums in the middle of the night, because my Elvis got all the other Vegas Elvises to be on the look-out for you."

She gives Darren a wide-eyed look. "That explains a lot!"

I frown at her. "Yeah, well, I've been all over the Strip chasing down tips that cost me fifty bucks each about where you'd been. And when I finally figured out you were inside *this* place, I stole some catering shirts and trays of food so we could sneak in the back door because we'd already been booted out the *front* door. But we still got chased down by security Gorillas, and when I *did* find you and figured out who this guy is, all you could do is tell me to watch the show! Like I care about a concert?" I turn to Darren. "No offense, but I don't want a rock star dad. I've already got a diva mom."

"Samantha!" my mom gasps, and I can tell—she's going to hate me for the rest of my life.

But when I look back at Darren, there's a little grin tugging at one side of his mouth. He's also sort of checking me over—my high-tops, my skateboard, my grungy jeans—and his eyes are definitely twinkling.

Not like he thinks I'm a joke.

More that he's decided he *likes* me.

Then Drumsticks chuckles and says, "I know you gotta do a paternity test, but, dude, that girl is yours."

Darren eyes him and grins. "A real Troublemaker, huh?"

"A paternity test?" Heather gasps. "Are they saying he's your . . ."

And that's when I actually *look* at Darren Cole.

First it's his eyes.

Then it's his teeth.

And then something clicks and I can just tell.

He really is my dad.

It's a weird take-your-breath-away, knock-your-knees-out feeling, and I can see that he's just been hit with it, too.

I really am his daughter.

All of a sudden I don't know what to say, what to do, or what to *think*, so I just stand there like an idiot, staring at him, and he just stands there, staring at me.

Then finally, real softly, he says, "It's nice to meet you, Samantha."

I nod and choke out, "It's Sammy. With a *y*."

The corner of his mouth tugs up again. "No heart on an *i* for you, huh?"

I give a little grin back. "Exactly."

He puts out a hand and says, "Well, I'm Darren. With two *r*'s." But as I'm shaking his hand, Heather cuts in with "He's your *dad*? You're her *dad*? When did this happen? How did— What is going *on*?" She squints at me. "And if he's your dad, then . . . This doesn't make any sense! Who *have* you been living with? And what's there to blackmail?"

I might have said, Wouldn't you like to know! or pulled a Lana and said, Can we please talk about this later? only right then someone walks through the door.

Someone who does not belong in Las Vegas.

Or at the House of Blues.

And absolutely positively not at a rock band's after-party.

"Grams?" I gasp, and then Hudson appears behind her, followed by . . .

"Casey?" Heather gasps.

So okay. Any minute I know I'm going to wake up on the couch in the Senior Highrise with my cat sleeping on my head giving me weird dreams. I mean, there's no way this can be reality. And something about understanding that gives me this huge wave of relief. Of course! The whole *trip* has been a dream! The Elvis Army, teaming up with Heather, sneaking into the House of Blues, Darren Cole being my dad . . .

It's all just a dream!

Hallucinations from suffocation!

All I have to do is wake up and, *poof,* it'll be over.

So when Grams sees me and goes, "Oh, thank God!" and Lady Lana sees *her* and cries, "Oh God, no!" I just smile. Serenely. Calmly.

I'm onto this.

It's just a dream.

And when Heather gasps again and says, "Oh my God! You live in that funky seniors' building with *her*?" I just keep smiling.

It's only a dream.

But then Casey's there, hugging me, and he's warm and strong and feels so *real.*

"Am I dreaming?" I ask in his ear, and I can feel my smile start to fade.

He laughs. "No."

But in a dream that's exactly what he'd say, right?

And then everybody starts talking all at once.

Just like they do in dreams.

And somehow Casey eases aside my backpack and

skateboard and he and Heather and I wind up in our own little zone where the two of them have a conversation about moms and dads and who said and did what. They're not fighting. Just talking. In a big, excited blur of words.

Somewhere in the middle of them talking I pinch myself—which actually really hurts—and I wake up to the fact that this is *not* a dream.

Casey really is here.

Darren Cole really is my father.

And Casey just said—

"What?" I ask.

"My mom says it's fine that we see each other."

My jaw drops. "She *did*?"

"She says to tell you thanks."

"She *did*?" I ask again.

And what that means is that the only thing standing in our way is . . .

We both look at Heather, who puts her hands up and says, "Do *not* make me say it. This whole thing is way too weird as it is. I'm *not* going to say it."

I eye her. "So what happened in Vegas . . . ?"

"What *did* happen in Vegas, anyway?" Casey asks. "All I know is Mom's talking to Dad, and Darren Cole's your father." He puts a hand to his head like just the thought might blow his mind apart. "Darren Cole!"

I heave a huge, puffy-cheeked sigh. "We definitely need a new song."

He laughs. "No kidding." Then he says, "And all that's plenty crazy enough, but *you* two?" He looks back and forth between Heather and me. "What happened?"

Heather and I kind of shrug and sneak looks at each other, and at the same time we both say, "We teamed up."

"Whoa."

"So?" I ask her after we've stood around all awkward for a minute.

She frowns. "I don't know, all right? It was easier when I hated you." She looks at her brother and finally says to both of us through her teeth, "I'm at my very first after-party, okay? I want to *meet* people. Can we just talk about this later?"

I shrug. "Sure." But when she takes off, Casey stands on his toes and calls out, "Hey, Troublemakers!" Then he points to his sister and says, "She's only thirteen, okay?"

"I hate you!" Heather yells back at him.

Which for some reason makes all the Troublemakers laugh and makes me feel like I've finally, *finally* gotten back to an edge of reality.

TWENTY-SIX

Somewhere in the middle of the strangeness that was the Troublemakers' after-party, it dawned on me that I'd been really harsh on Grams. She'd known the real reason my mother was coming to Las Vegas and was just trying to hold it all together for a little while longer.

I tried to block out my guilt over how I'd treated her, because I also needed to apologize to Casey for being such an awful girlfriend. And even though I was interested in everything he'd told me—like how Grams and Hudson had tracked him down and how they'd all pieced together what had happened and then how he'd stowed away in Hudson's car and hadn't shown himself until it was way too late to turn back—in the back of my mind I was fretting about Grams.

But then he says, "Your mom was actually trying to do the right thing, Sammy," and I kind of snap out of it.

"How's *that*?"

"Well, I overheard a bunch of stuff before they knew I was there."

"Like *what*?"

"He . . ."

His voice just trails off, so I ask, "He who?"

"Do you want me to call him Darren or your dad?"

"Darren!"

"Okay. Well, his first album was just getting traction, he was touring, she was nuts about him and went out to see him on the road to break the news about you and discovered he was doing the typical rock star thing. So they got in a huge fight and broke up, and she was *done* with him." He eyed me. "Single moms scraping by have a tough time chasing their Hollywood dream. But your grandmother promised she'd help raise you . . . which is why your mom felt like she could leave you at the Highrise."

Hearing this from Casey was somehow easier than hearing it from Mom.

Or Grams.

From them, things always sound like excuses. From Casey?

They sounded . . . tragic.

Betrayed by the love of her life, woman returns home to have baby, whose eyes and smile are just like her cad dad's.

I wanted to change the subject fast because I always seem to get burned when I find some sympathy for my mother. And since Casey was just holding my hands, kind of waiting for me to say something, what I said was "I'm sorry I've been such a rotten girlfriend."

"What are you talking about?"

"It's Valentine's Day? Or at least it was? I stood you up, I didn't get you a present. . . . I was really *possessed* about my mom getting married when I should have been thinking about you." I give him a guilty look. "I tried to call you. Really, I did."

"My cell?"

"I thought your mom confiscated that."

"She did, but I knew where she stashed it, so I dug it up before I stashed myself in Hudson's car." He grins. "Which is how I got in touch with my mom and how I found out about your talk with her." He digs something out of his jeans pocket, saying, "So you managing to get her to say it's okay for us to see each other is a *way* better present than this"—he loops a chain around my neck—"but this is all I have."

On the chain is a little skeleton key.

And a silver heart.

They're both tarnished, with cool scrollwork . . . like they've been around forever and will last forever.

My eyes brim full of tears. "This is the coolest necklace ever."

Now, at that moment I had completely forgotten my guilt over Grams. But then I hear, "Excuse me for butting in . . . ," and when I look up, there's Hudson. "Oh, Hudson, I'm so sorry!" I tell him. "I can't believe you drove all the way here! And in Jester? I didn't think you were supposed to drive classic cars that far."

"The car and I held up just fine. Your grandmother?" He cocks his head and gives a tisk. "That's another story."

"I gotta go talk to her," I tell Casey, but then I notice she's standing with my mother and Darren and they're all looking pretty glum. "Uh . . . maybe later."

"No," Hudson tells me. "You should go now."

If there's one adult in my life I can count on to always give me good advice, it's Hudson Graham. So I nod, and I'm about to head over when Casey says, "Wait up." So I do while he reads a text. "Sorry, but I gotta go," he says. "Mom wants Heather and me to meet her at the hotel room right away."

"Glad you've got your phone," I tell him as he sends a text back. Then we give each other a big hug, and in my ear he says, "I guess I'll see you back in Santa Martina?"

"Don't let your mother drive too fast," I whisper back.

He gives me a quick kiss, then goes to pry his sister away while I head over to where Grams is still standing with Lady Lana and Darren Cole.

"I'm sorry, Grams," I tell her straight up, trying to focus on just her. "It was a big hodgepodge of emergencies and misunderstandings and—"

"Samantha, I'm done with hodgepodges of emergencies and misunderstandings. My heart just can't take this anymore. It is too exhausting for me to be looking after a teenager."

"Especially such a troublemaker," Darren says with a grin.

Now, I can tell he's just trying to lighten things up a little, but obviously he's clueless about how serious this is sounding. "Hey!" I say, pointing at him. "You stay out of it! If you hadn't gone and broken my mother's heart, none of this would be happening." He looks at me like, Ouch, and my mother stares at me like, Wow, so I look at *her* and say, "Casey just told me." Then I turn to Grams and drop my voice when I ask, "What are you saying?" 'cause my gut is all topsy-turvy over what I'm *afraid* she's saying.

She pinches her eyes and shakes her head. "You staying with me was never supposed to be long-term. You and your mother will have to figure it out."

"No!" I cry. "Please, Grams! Please! I promise I won't stow away in any more cars or jump on any more planes or . . . or do anything I'm not supposed to!"

"I can't do it anymore, Samantha. Now that Heather knows? It's unworkable."

"Grams! No! Heather and I are having a truce. Things will be fine! You're just tired. It's one in the morning! You drove a long, long, long, long, long, long way! We'll get a room, we'll get some sleep, and we'll talk about it tomorrow, okay?"

She shakes her head and sighs. "Where's Hudson?" And all of a sudden there he is, putting an arm around her. "I'm glad you're safe," she says to me. "I was never so worried in my life." Then she strokes Hudson's cheek and says, "Let's go."

"What? Wait! You can't go!"

Hudson gives me a reassuring look and whispers, "She's exhausted."

But I can tell—this is different than all the times before.

Grams means it.

And then they do go.

"They have rooms at the MGM," my mother says, holding me back as I go to chase after them. "I'll get us one there, too, and we'll go see them in the morning."

And since I'm now crying and being the total after-party

downer, I tell her, "I'm going to go sit out there for a while."

"Out where?"

"I don't know! Somewhere out *there*," I tell her, pointing through the door. Then I look at Darren and say, "I'm sorry. I really am. I know this is weird for you, too."

All he does is give a little nod—probably 'cause he's already learned that if he *says* something, I'll bite him for it. But two steps out the door, there he is, walking next to me.

"Brave guy," I tell him with a scowl.

"I may have been young and reckless," he tells me, "but I'm no deadbeat dad."

And that's when a thought slams me upside the head. It's so big and so *complicating* that for a split second I forget everything else. "Are you saying I have . . . brothers and sisters? Or you know, *step*brothers and -sisters?"

"No!" He laughs. "At least not that I know of!"

I eye him.

Like, Very funny, you jerk.

"Look, it wasn't like that with your mother. We were in love. Being on the road . . . ?" He shrugs. "I can't make excuses for my behavior back then, but I *have* grown up some."

We're at the edge of the stage now, so I sit down with my feet dangling, and so does he. "Well, how many *wives* have you had?"

He gives me a long, even look. "None."

"None?"

"None." Then kinda softly he adds, "Nobody ever

compared to your mother." We sit there quiet for a min-ute, and finally he says, "I've got good reasons to be mad at her for not telling me about you, but"—he gives a hope-less little shrug—"it's just so good to see her." He eyes me. "Still, I do wish I'd known."

"Me, too," I tell him, but while I'm saying it, it flashes through my mind that if I *had* known . . . if my mom *had* told him when I was younger . . . I wouldn't know Grams like I do.

And my friends would all be . . . different.

And I would never have met Casey!

"I'm not moving to Vegas," I blurt out. "Or Hollywood!"

He laughs. "Well, we've got to figure out *something*." Then he adds, "I want to get to know you, Sammy."

My eyes are all of a sudden stinging again. "Don't say stuff like that! For all I know, this is just another lie."

"There's no doubt that my lawyer's going to make me do a DNA test, but everything about it makes sense." He laughs. "Besides, look at you! Listen to you!" He shakes his head. "Marko's right—you're definitely my kid." He kind of grins and says, "Your poor mother."

Before I can stop myself, I'm shoving him and laugh-ing. "Hey!"

"So I'm *thinking*. . . ."

"Uh-oh."

"Why uh-oh?"

I look at him. "Everyone always tells me they know they're in trouble when I say that."

He chuckles. "Yeah, well, see what I mean?"

"So? Let's hear it."

"I understand your birthday's coming up."

And out of my mouth pops, "I don't want a pony!"

His eyebrows go flying. "Who said anything about a pony?"

"Isn't that what all rock star dads give their daughters?"

"Dumb ones, maybe," he says, and he's grinning.

But I'm serious. "Look, I don't want anything from you, okay? I've got everything I need in Grams' bottom dresser drawer."

"That's very rock 'n' roll of you."

"Stop that!"

"No, really. That's the heart of rock 'n' roll—all the 'stuff' just perverts that and ruins it."

"So good. Don't buy me anything."

He snorts. "I wasn't planning to."

"Oh."

"But I was thinking that I'd really like to *be* there."

"For my birthday?"

He sorta studies me. "I missed the first thirteen?" Then he adds, "And maybe we can plan to do something over your spring break?"

I want to tell him that that sounds nice—and it does.

But it also sounds . . . awkward.

What would we say to each other?

What would we do?

"Look," he finally says. "There's obviously a lot we have to work through. What do *you* think? I can see you're pretty upset."

"What I'm *most* upset about is Grams. I mean, Mom's

been flaky, you've been a mystery, but through everything I could always count on Grams. *She's* my family." All of a sudden there's this huge lump in my throat, and my eyes are stinging *again*. "Maybe I finally know who you are, but if it cost me Grams?" I shake my head. "I need to find a way to fix things with her."

We just sit there, me battling the lump in my throat, him quiet, until finally he gets up and holds out a hand. "Well, let's go figure that out, then."

I stare at him a minute, then take his hand and let him help me back on my feet.

TWENTY-SEVEN

My mother got a room with two beds, but they were right next to each other, so I chose the couch. And even though I was wiped out, I didn't fall asleep until about five in the morning because I couldn't stop thinking about Grams and wondering what in the world I was going to do.

I heard my mom rustling around in the morning, but I just rolled over and went back to sleep, and when I woke up again, it was noon and she was gone.

I needed a shower bad, so I dragged myself into the bathroom and took a long, hot, muscle-melting one. And since I hadn't brought much in the way of extra clothes, I wound up raiding a pair of jeans and an amazingly soft hoodie from my mother's suitcase.

A little big, but definitely comfy.

Next to the phone I found a blueberry muffin and a note from my mom telling me to call her cell. So I did, but there was really only one thing I wanted to know. "Have you talked to Grams?"

"Your dad and I did."

Hearing her say it like that was too much, too early, but I just sort of shook it off and said, "And?"

"Darren offered to set her up in a house."

"As in *buy* her a house?"

"Yes."

"Where?"

"In Santa Martina. But your grandmother said no."

I took a deep breath and let it out. "Of course she said no. Grams isn't the kind of person you can bribe."

"It wasn't a *bribe*. Darren knows you want to stay in Santa Martina, and getting her out of the Highrise was one solution."

"It's not a solution to her not wanting to take care of me anymore. And she already has a place to live."

"Well, you told your dad you don't want to move to Hollywood or Las Vegas, so what are we going to do?"

"Where is she?" I asked quietly. "I want to go talk to her."

"She's at the spa."

"The *spa*? What's she doing at the *spa*?"

"Recovering?"

Something about that made me feel worse than ever. I'd driven my poor grandmother, who never pampers herself, into the massaging arms of a *spa*? "How long's *that* going to take?"

"An hour? Maybe two?"

"Well, what room is she staying in? And where's Hudson?"

"She's in seven twenty, and he's in seven twenty-two." Then she asks, "Are you all right on your own for a little while?"

I snort. "I've had lots of practice."

251

"Samantha, please."

"Well, come on, Mom!"

"I'm sorry. I'm sorry about all of this. You think I'm not filled with regret? I'm just trying to figure out how we can move forward from here without more damage. The easy thing would be for you to come live with me, but—"

"You don't even have a job!"

"That's a separate issue. And I *will* get a job. The point is, I'm trying to figure out what's best for *you*." She takes a choppy breath and chokes out, "I love you, Samantha. Even if that's hard for you to believe."

And on that dramatic note, she hangs up.

I sit there a minute thinking, then dial Hudson's room. No answer.

So I call Grams' room, even though I know she's not there, and I leave a pathetic, stuttery message, begging her to forgive me and let me come talk to her. "We're in room eleven-eleven, and I'm going to just wait here for you to call me." Then I tell her I love her and go to hang up, but at the last minute I pull the phone back up and say, "*Please* call me."

And *then* I hang up.

After sitting there for a few more minutes thinking, I call Casey and find out that he's already on his way back to Santa Martina, crammed in the backseat of Candi's sports car with Heather. "What's going on with your parents?" I ask.

"Can't really discuss that now."

"Can you do yes and no questions? Are they getting back together?"

"Too early to say." Then he drops his voice and says, "Everyone's being weirdly nice. I don't even know these people!"

Then I hear a female voice go, "Hi, Sammy!"

"Holy cow, was that Heather?"

"Yup. She's still flying high about last night."

"Are you guys anywhere near Vegas?"

"No. We've been on the road at least two hours."

I laugh. "Well, I guess what happened is not staying in Vegas."

He laughs, too. "Apparently not!"

"Okay. Well, I'll let you get back to your *family*. Lucky dog."

"Wait! What's going on with yours?"

And because I don't want him worrying about me when things are obviously going well for him, I laugh and say, "Oh, it's a bigger mess than ever, but we're working on figuring it out." Then I tell him, "Hey, I need to call Marissa, okay? She's clueless about any of this, and I want her to find out from me first."

"Right. Okay! I'll see you at home."

"See you at home!"

So I hang up and call Marissa, but the minute I have her on the line, she attacks me with "Yes, I know you got to meet Darren Cole! Yes, I know you snuck into the House of Blues! Yes, I know you ditched security! Yes, I know you got to see the show from the front row! Heather keeps posting online about it, and she's making it sound like you guys are best friends!"

I can feel myself getting hotter and hotter, but then

it hits me that something's missing from what Marissa "knows."

"Did she post anything about Darren Cole being my dad?"

"Did she . . . *what*?"

"Well, sit down," I tell her, " 'cause he is."

So I spend the next *hour* catching her up for real, and when we're finally down to "What are you going to do?" and "I don't know!" I switch over to *her* problems. "So what's happening with your dad?"

"Ohhhh," she moans, and then launches into how Hudson had taken Mikey over to her uncle Bruce's because of the emergency trip to Las Vegas, and how Mikey had spilled the beans about the gambling, and how after a huge brothers' blowout over that, her mom had caught her dad trying to gamble online. "It's over, Sammy. They're selling the house, and Mom says she wants a divorce."

Now, normally when Marissa is in crisis mode, you can tell right away because her voice is frantic and up a notch and all twisted with stress. But now she sounds all matter-of-fact. Almost monotone. So I ask, "How can you be so *calm*?"

"I'm just wiped out, Sammy. I can't stop my dad from gambling, and I can't blame my mom for wanting to get divorced."

I let that soak in. "So what's going to happen with you and Mikey?"

"We'll be with Mom, but I don't know where. She's

talking about making a clean break and starting fresh some-where new."

"Like, away from Santa Martina?"

"Yup."

"No! You've got to talk her out of that! What would I do without you? And think about Mikey! It would kill him to leave Hudson!"

She sighs. "I know."

"So don't let her move out of town!"

She hesitates, then asks, "You're coming home with Hudson and your grandmother, right?"

"I hope so! I thought we'd be driving home today, but I think probably tomorrow."

She sighs. "I really, really want to talk to Hudson."

"I know, huh?" And then it hits me. "You thinking about seeing if you and Mikey can stay with him?"

"Maybe we could rent his place in back?"

"All of you?"

"Yeah."

"Have you been inside it? It's awfully small." But I'm also thinking that I *want* it to be too small for them, 'cause it would actually be perfect for *me*.

We're both quiet a minute, and then she says, "Isn't it funny?"

"What?"

"I used to be rich and have the picture-book family, and now I'm broke and my family's a disaster."

"What's so funny about that?"

"Because you used to be broke with no family, and now?"

"I still don't have a family."

"Sure you do. From what you said, I can tell—it'll all come together."

"But I don't *want* to live with them! Not either of them! I want to live with Grams."

"On a couch. In a run-down old folks' home."

"Yes!"

"You've outgrown that, Sammy. It's time to move on."

"You don't move on from someone you love! I *love* Grams. She is the strongest, nicest, most caring person I've ever known!"

"Sammy, she'll always love you, whether you live with her or not."

"She's furious with me!"

She laughs. "That's temporary. Just keep trying. You'll patch things up with her." She sighs. "Tell Hudson we miss him big-time!"

So I get off the phone, and right away I dial Grams' room and leave another pathetic message, then call Hudson's room. And when he doesn't answer, either, I'm forced to call my mother, but she informs me that Grams is now getting her nails done.

"She's getting a *manicure?*"

"A mani-pedi. It'll take a while."

"But . . . Grams doesn't get her *nails* done."

"All I can tell you is what she told me. She's still miffed at the way I handled things, so I'm just letting her cool off."

"So we're not going home today?"

"Definitely not going home today." Then she asks, "Are you up for seeing your dad?"

"No! I'm up for taking a nap."

"A nap? You've only been awake for a couple of hours!"

"Yeah, well, I had a really intense day yesterday, and I'm still wiped out."

"You're probably starving. Why don't we take you out for lunch?"

"We? As in you and Darren?"

"Yes."

"I'll get my own food."

"Samantha, no. I'll bring you something. What do you like?"

A question she has to ask because of course she has no idea. So I tell her, "Mac 'n' cheese and salsa. Or chicken salad with grapes. Or a tuna wrap with kalamata olives and cucumbers." And before she can say anything about my food choices, I ask, "How come you can get in touch with Hudson and Grams and I can't?"

"They call me. And where am I supposed to get a tuna wrap with kalamata olives and cucumbers?"

"Well, could you *please* tell them to call *me* next time they call you?"

"Sure. But what about the wrap?"

I sigh. "I don't care about the wrap. I really just want a nap."

So I get off the phone, try Hudson's again, hang up, and since I really do feel totally wiped out, I actually do take a nap.

What wakes me up is not Grams calling.

What wakes me up is my mother coming through the door.

"Nooooo," I moan, 'cause she's got Darren with her. "I'm in a horrible mood," I tell him. "You probably don't want to be here."

He gives me a hopeful look and hoists some plastic bags. "We brought lunch?"

And that's when I realize I'm starving.

I sit up and rake back my hair. "What about Grams?"

My mom starts laying out the food on the coffee table. "She's getting her hair done."

"Getting her *hair* done? Doesn't she know I'm dying to talk to her?"

"I told her, Samantha, but you know how she can be."

"How *she* can be? She's the way she is because you're the way *you* are!"

"Hmm," she says, like a fully coronated diva. "Have you ever thought that maybe I'm the way I am because she's the way *she* is?"

"Grams is nothing like you!"

She raises one perfectly plucked eyebrow at me.

That's all.

Just an eyebrow.

Then she says, "Let's eat, shall we?" which is one of her ninety-six ways of changing the subject.

There's nothing resembling mac 'n' cheese and salsa. Or chicken salad with grapes. Or a tuna wrap with kalamata olives and cucumbers. Or even PB&J. But there is an egg salad sandwich, so I take that and an apple juice.

"Thanks," I tell Darren in a very grumbly way.

My mother reaches into her vast catalog of disapproving looks and shoots one at me, but Darren doesn't seem fazed. He just shoves a bag of salt and vinegar chips over and says, "Goes great with egg salad."

Which for some reason takes the edge off the way I'm feeling.

Then he adds, "So does Frank's, but we don't have any, so . . ."

"Frank's?"

"Hot sauce," he says, and when he can tell I've never heard of it, he explains. "It's like Tabasco but infinitely better." He gives my mom a little grin. "Some of us can't take the heat, but I slather. Great on carrots, too."

"Hot sauce is?" I ask him.

"That's right." He takes a bite of some kind of cold-cut sandwich, and after a few chews he says, "We could definitely use some Frank's here."

So okay. Now I'm actually smiling 'cause this guy is . . . well, let's just say he's *way* easier to be around than my mother. So I dig into my sandwich, too, and the vinegar chips give it some kick. "That *is* good," I tell him, then shake the chip bag at him.

"Thanks," he says with a grin.

So Darren and I eat bad sandwiches with good chips while my mother takes dainty bites from some fruity-looking yogurt cup. And I've just polished off the first half of my sandwich when I notice that Darren's trying to figure out how to say something.

"What?" I ask him.

He eyes my mom, then focuses on me. "Lana and I were bouncing around ideas about ways I could get to know you better." His eyebrows twitch up and he gives me a little look. "Unless you're not ready for that."

Maybe it was the vinegar chips talking, but I said, "Sounds good."

He and my mom exchange another look, and then he says, "Cool." He takes a deep breath. "We have some options, but the one that sounds like it might be the most fun for you would be joining me on a cruise where the band's been hired to play—"

"A *cruise?*" I look at him, horrified. "The guy who wrote 'Waiting for Rain to Fall' and 'Dead Weather' and 'Heal This Heart' is playing a *cruise?*"

"Wow," he says, studying me. "As if that decision wasn't hard enough."

It takes me a second, but I finally look away. "Sorry."

And we're all quiet a minute, but then he turns it around. "So," he says with half a grin, "you know my music?"

"You have no idea," I mutter.

"And you *like* it?"

"My boyfriend introduced me to you." I eye my mother, and she looks away quick. "So yeah," I tell him. "I like your music." I shake my head. "Which is totally awkward."

He laughs. "Yeah, I can see that."

And then my mother's phone rings.

I jump and cry, "Grams!" Only it comes out more like "Mmoums!" because I'd just taken a bite of sandwich.

"Lana Keyes," my mom answers, sounding stupidly official. And then she makes little noises for, like, two minutes while I sit there wiggling my hand for the phone. And finally, *finally* she says, "That's all fine and understandable, and I support all of that, but Samantha is right here and desperate to talk to you."

And then she's quiet for another thirty seconds before she says, "Mother? Mother, please . . ." Then she sighs and clicks off.

"Seriously?" I gasp. "She wouldn't talk to me?"

My mother looks away. "I'm sorry."

"Where is she?" I ask, 'cause I'm ready to track her down and *make* her talk to me.

"Shopping."

"*Shopping*? For what?"

My mother shrugs. "It's Las Vegas. The possibilities are endless."

"But Grams doesn't shop! And how can she be *shopping* when she knows I'm miserable?"

My mother sighs again. "She needs a little *her* time."

"*Her* time?" I throw my hands up in the air because for the first time ever Grams is acting like my *mother*. And let me tell you, this makes my head turn back into one weird, muddled mess. I mean, not being able to reach Grams is one thing. Having her shut me down cold when she knows I'm desperate to talk to her and am *right there* is something else. Because I don't care what my mother says, Grams is *not* like her. She's caring and supportive and giving and self*less*.

But . . . how could she know I'm totally miserable and

still go to the spa, get a mani-pedi, get her hair done, and go *shopping*?

How?

And that's when something Pete had said goes jailhouse-rocking through my brain.

"Ohmygod!" I cry, jumping up.

Lady Lana recoils like she's just spotted blood. "What?"

"She's getting married!"

"What?" she says again. "Who?"

"Grams!" I dash from here to there across the room, until I wind up back where I started. "Come on! We have to go!"

"Go where?"

"To the chapel!"

"What chapel? Samantha, calm down. Why do you think she's getting married?"

"Come on." I yank her out of her seat. "There's no way I'm missing this wedding!"

TWENTY-EIGHT

The MGM's chapel was open, and there was a woman at the reception desk. The place was all marbly and fancy, but I marched my high-tops right in anyway.

"What time is the wedding for Hudson Graham and Rita Keyes?" I asked.

Mom was behind me and started making little cooing noises to the woman about excusing the intrusion.

Darren was smart enough to stay outside.

"Seven-thirty," the woman said, and, *ka-thunk,* my mom's jaw hit the ground.

"Told you," I snarled at my mom as I dragged her back outside.

"She was right," my mom gasps to Darren. Then she looks at me and says, "How could she do this without telling us?"

I laugh. "I'm sure she's *planning* to tell us. *Some*day." Then I switch gears. "But forget about that—we've got work to do!"

"Work to do? What do you mean?"

I spread my arms out. "I need a dress! And shoes!

And we need to get cans! And a JUST MARRIED sign for Jester!"

"Who's Jester?" Darren asks.

"Hudson's car! It's a 1960 sienna rose Cadillac with whitewall tires and tons of chrome."

"That's what he drove to get here? A vintage Cadillac?"

"Yup." And then I get a great idea. I put my hand out to my mother. "Hand me your phone."

So she does and I dial and pretty soon I'm hearing, "You've reached the King!"

"Pete! It's Sammy! How would you like to cruise the Strip tonight in a 1960 pink Cadillac? It's pristine."

He hesitates. "What's the hitch?"

"It's more who's getting hitched. I'm happy to pay you."

"You found her? I thought you *didn't* want her to get married!"

"I found her, but it's actually my grandmother who's getting hitched."

"Whoa, little mama, you've had one complicated weekend."

"No kidding! But you'll do it?"

"Sure!"

"Okay! The ceremony's at seven-thirty at the MGM wedding chapel."

"Small service, I take it?"

"Oh yeah."

"So it'll take about half an hour tops. I'll be there before eight."

"Thanks! And, uh, Pete?"

"Yes?"

"Don't bring the Army. I think one Elvis is all my grandmother can handle."

He laughs. "Right. See you soon, little mama!"

I hand the phone back to my mother, who asks me, "You're hiring an Elvis, and you *flew* here. Where are you getting all this money?"

"Uh . . . it's reward money."

"Reward money."

"Yeah."

"For what?"

"Well . . . it's a long story involving a guy named Justice Jack, a pink trailer, some junkyard dogs, and a dairy farm, but basically, someone stole the softball statue out of the foyer of City Hall, and I helped get it returned. So I got a cut of the reward money." And since she and Darren are just *staring* at me, I go, "Are we getting ready for a wedding, or what?"

Darren says, "I'll help with the cans," but my mom cuts in with "Nobody does that anymore."

We both look at her. "On a vintage pink Cadillac?" Darren says. "It's perfect!"

I laugh. "Exactly!" And I can't help it; I give him a big ol' smile.

Lady Lana shakes her head. "What have I done?"

So for the next hour we race around buying stuff and decorating Hudson's car—which was pretty easy to find, even in the massive parking structure. And by the time seven-thirty rolled around, I was wearing a dress and, as Grams would say, a pair of "real" shoes. The dress wasn't fancy—just a simple blue thing with little flowers on the collar—but I knew Grams would love it. I also found her a bracelet with blue stones. They were fake, but they looked good, and come on! You don't get *that* much for returning an ugly bronze statue!

Darren bought chocolates and flowers, and Lady Lana managed to get a set of hankies embroidered on the spot: Hudson + Rita in a heart.

They were awesome.

Then we raced downstairs and waited outside the chapel.

And waited.

And waited.

And finally I ask, "What time is it?"

"Seven-forty," Darren tells me.

I put out my hand to Lady Lana. "Phone."

So she hands it over, and pretty soon Hudson is answering his room phone.

I don't even bother to say hello. "Did she get cold feet?"

"Sammy?"

"Yes. Is she there all dressed and ready to go?"

"How did you—" He chuckles. "Of course you figured it out."

"Well, we're down at the chapel waiting."

"You are? That's wonderful! Because after she heard your messages, she decided she didn't want to go through with it without you, but she thought it was too late to ask you."

"Well, me and Mom and Darren are all here, so get down here! We have flowers and presents and I'm in a *dress*, for crying out loud! So tell her there's no backing out. Oh! And make sure you bring your car keys!"

"We'll be right down."

So I hand back the phone and march into the chapel and tell the staff that they're dealing with old people and they'll just have to be a little patient. And after a short wait, *poof*, there's Hudson in a top hat and tails and Grams looking stunning in a cream-colored dress.

All of a sudden I'm a silly, gooshy-faced girl, sniffling and crying and telling Grams she looks gorgeous and putting the "something blue" on her wrist and telling her that I love her more than she could ever know.

"I'm glad you're here," she says softly, then gives me the sweetest smile.

Hudson puts out an elbow for Grams and says, "You ready, sweetheart?"

Sweetheart!

He called her sweetheart!

I start streaming at the eyes all over again.

And then in they go to get married.

I cried through most of the wedding. I knew Grams was starting a new life without me, and I *didn't* know what I was going to do, but seeing two of the people I love most in the world get married was awesome. I was so happy for Grams. And Hudson. They had had kind of a rocky romance, but she had been sweet on him from early on, and the more time they had spent together, the easier it was to see that they really were right for each other.

Perfect, in fact.

And I guess what made me so emotional was that Hudson already felt like family.

He was the guy I went to for advice.

He was the guy I could trust with my secrets and troubles and worries.

He was my *friend*.

And now he was my gramps!

Although, actually, we were going to have to talk about that. Maybe he'd still want me to call him Hudson.

Maybe *I'd* still want to call him Hudson.

But then again, maybe not!

Anyway, after they'd said their "I dos" and were signing the paperwork, I got Hudson's keys from him and had Darren take Pete around to where the car was so he could pull it up to the lobby entrance.

Grams was absolutely glowing as we led her away from the chapel to the car, and random people cheered and whistled and yelled congratulations as we made our way through the casino and the lobby.

I was a little worried about Hudson's reaction to Elvis behind the wheel of his car, but when he saw what we'd done, he said, "Brilliant!" and laughed like a little boy.

Grams turned to Mom and me and said, "This was all so thoughtful. Thank you."

"Samantha was behind most of it."

"Isn't she always?" Grams says, smiling at me.

"I'm happy for you, Mom," my mother tells her, and after they've hugged, Grams hugs me, too, and says, "Thank you, Samantha."

I start crying again. "I love you, Grams. I'm sorry I've been so much trouble."

She holds my cheeks and says, "What's a little trouble with a heart as big as yours?"

By now Hudson's car is causing kind of a traffic jam, so Pete stretches out and calls, "Come on, baby, let's play house!"

Hudson laughs and gives Elvis a thumbs-up, then helps Grams into the backseat and passes her the box of chocolates and the flowers before hurrying around to get in the other side.

"Have fun!" we call, then wave as Elvis eases the car forward and the cans start clanking behind them.

And there they go.

And then they stop.

"What's wrong?" I call, because Hudson's getting out of the car.

"Seems we're missing something," he says back.

"What?"

He grins. "Our family." Then he makes a grand sweeping motion, which can only mean one thing.

Get in!

The three of us all look at each other, and when Darren says, "Me, too?" I tell him, "I can't be the only trouble-maker in the family—come on!"

So Darren and my mom sit up with Elvis, and I pile in back next to Grams.

Then we roll out of the driveway and into the bright lights of Las Vegas, Grams holding Hudson's hand on the left.

And mine on the right.

Turn the page for a sneak peek at
Sammy Keyes and the Killer Cruise.

PROLOGUE

I look back on things I've done and wonder . . . why didn't I see that coming?

Why didn't I know that was a bad idea?

Why didn't someone *warn* me?

Grams would tell you she *does* warn me and that the question should really be, Why don't I *listen?*

Which, yeah, I admit, is usually the case.

But not this time. This time *I* thought it was a bad idea. This time I warned Grams and my mother and Hudson and anyone else who told me it was a good idea that it was a bad idea.

This time *they* didn't listen.

Which is how I wound up on a cruise ship with a dad I barely knew, an endless buffet of party animals, and a family of creepy millionaires.

Happy birthday to me.

ONE

I was allowed to bring one friend. And since Marissa McKenze has been my best friend since third grade, and since it looks like she'll be moving to Ohio in June because her mom's lined up a job there and who knows how long it'll be before I'll get to do anything with her again after that, and since I wasn't allowed to bring Casey because he's my boyfriend and it would have been "inappropriate," and since my other good friend, Holly, thought cruising sounded like a nightmare, the choice was easy.

Marissa.

Even Mrs. McKenze was for it, and she's never for anything that has to do with her daughter spending time with me. According to her, I'm "hazardous."

And yet, there we were, at the Long Beach dock with our luggage and passports, about to cruise to Mexico.

Actually, I think Mrs. McKenze being okay with the trip had more to do with Darren Cole being my dad than her daughter having one last adventure with her best friend.

He seems to have that effect on middle-aged women.

Something about the shaggy hair and guitar makes them lose their minds.

Or, at least, their common sense.

Him sending a car service to get us to the dock didn't hurt, either. Mrs. McKenze actually gasped when she heard it was how we were getting to Los Angeles and I could tell I was suddenly a friend she *wanted* her daughter to hang with instead of the "hazard" I'd been before. Why a week away with a musician didn't register as a hazard to her was beyond me, but like I said, common sense didn't apply.

Marissa was over the moon about going on the cruise. She'd been on cruises before with her family, pre-financial meltdown/divorce. "It's awesome, Sammy. You have no idea! You can't even picture it, it's so amazing! It's like twenty stories of a Las Vegas resort steaming through the ocean!"

Which, having been to Las Vegas, didn't help to sell me on the idea at *all*.

And since she hadn't actually met my dad in person yet, she'd blown the whole thing way out of proportion. People would ask us what we were doing over spring break and she'd say, "Sammy and I are going on a celebrity cruise!"

"It's not a celebrity cruise!" I'd tell her through my teeth.

"Sure it is! Your dad's a celebrity and he's playing on the cruise!"

"He's playing one night. That's all!"

But it was like she couldn't help herself. She kept letting it slip out until finally I told her, "Knock it off or stay home!"

Her eyes had gotten huge. "You wouldn't do that to me!"

"Yes, I would! The whole situation is embarrassing enough without you doing this!"

Which it was. It had only been about six weeks since I'd found out that my dad was Darren Cole of Darren Cole and the Troublemakers, and I was still pretty weirded out by it. Partly because going from being poor to finding out you're the daughter of a rock star puts you smack-dab in the middle of some really strange territory, and partly because people at school love to gossip, and Darren Cole being my father became Big News fast.

It was amazing to see how many new "friends" I suddenly had, too. People who'd made fun of me before were now all being nice to me.

Thanks, but no thanks.

When we're at the Long Beach dock waiting for Darren to show up and Marissa suddenly points and squeals, "There he *is*," I can tell she's going to be trouble. I grab her and get right in her face. "No squealing. No fawning. No gushing or gawking or . . . or fainting! He is just a guy. Just. A. Guy."

There are masses of people swarming around and checking their luggage at different stations, but when I look over to where Marissa had pointed, I spot Darren right away. Maybe it's the Louis Vuitton sunglasses. Or the blazer he has on instead of the beachy clothes so many other people are wearing.

Or maybe it's the boots.

Who wears boots on a cruise?

"Sammy!" he calls, flashing a great big smile.

He's got no luggage. No suitcase, no guitar, no nothing.

And that's when it hits me—he's not coming.

Something's come up and he can't make it.

I can feel myself get mad and hurt and withdrawn all at once.

Like I haven't had enough cancellations and gushing apologies and pathetic excuses from my diva mother.

But hey, just another reality check—I should be used to getting them handed to me by now.

"Sammy!" he calls again.

I do give him a nod, but Marissa doesn't catch it. "Why aren't you answering him?" she asks, and then does a big, dopey wave that people in Hawaii could have seen.

"We canceled?" I ask when he gets up to us.

He slips the Louis Vuittons down his nose and looks at me eye to eye. "Canceled? Why would we be canceled?"

"Where's your stuff?" I ask, looking around like, Hello, stuff . . . ?

"It's being loaded in with the band's gear." He has a quick conversation with our driver/escort and signs some papers, and then all of a sudden he calls out, "Marko! Marko, over here!"

Marissa whips around to look, then whips back and whispers, "Who's Marko?"

"The drummer," I tell her, and before you know it, he's standing right there in board shorts and a cool gray T, with his shaved head and little piratey earring, smiling from ear to ear, going, "Dude! The ship is *huge*."

Darren slaps his shoulder and checks him over with a grin. "You goin' on a cruise or something?"

"Dude, I am so ready!" Then he smiles at me and says, "Hey-yo, Sammy!"

Darren takes out a big envelope of paperwork from inside his sports coat. "Let the adventure begin!"

"Uh, I'm Marissa?" Marissa says, putting a hand out.

Darren pumps it. "Darren." He turns to Marko. "And this is my best friend and Troublemakin' timekeeper, Marko."

Marko shakes her hand and says, "Nice to meet you, Marissa." But as Darren starts to walk, she looks around a little and asks, "Aren't we waiting for the others?"

Darren looks over his shoulder at her. "The others?"

"The rest of the band?"

Darren smiles at her. "Glad you're on the lookout for trouble, but Drew and Cardillo aren't meeting up with us until later."

"Wow," Marissa whispers as Darren leads us to a line where we're supposed to turn over our luggage. "Is he your dad or what?"

"Shh!" Then I ask, "What do you mean?"

"His eyes, the way he smiles, the way he—"

"Shh!"

"How can you be so matter-of-fact about this? This is awesome!"

And I know she's right.

I know that it is.

And the truth is, I have butterflies.

Not nervous butterflies.

Happy butterflies.

I can't quite believe we're here, doing this. I can't quite believe that nothing's "come up," that nobody's flaked, and that I'm going on a cruise with . . . with my dad.

"Why are you crying?" Marissa whispers.

I shake it off. "I'm okay."

"You sure?"

I nod and roll my luggage up closer to Darren and Marko.

Let the adventure begin!